AF508417

Friends with Wings

Maxwell Pearl

ECHOBIRD
PRESS

Address inquiries in permission to:
Echobird Press, echobirdpress.com
ISBN 979-8-9863865-4-6 | ISBN 979-8-9863865-5-3 EPUB

Table of Contents

Introduction to this edition

I wrote this novel almost 10 years ago. I was a different person and a different writer then. There are some things I would change about the characters, but I didn't really have time – I am too busy with new work and new ideas. I removed this from sale when I changed my name and gender, because I didn't want novels with my old name still being sold. But I didn't want this novel to just die on my hard drive.

This novel has been slightly edited: mostly copy edits and better language and such. Nothing substantive has been changed, for better and for worse.

Journal Entry, January 10, 2136

I am alone and have been alone for one hundred days. Not really alone, of course. Zolweeva, Keeliza and all of their clan are gentle and generous, even though we don't really understand each other yet. All of the winged creatures that I've met have been kind and they are very curious about me.

They answer all my questions, and care for me, and they like to keep me company, but that hasn't made the loneliness go away. I think that they understand that being so alone is difficult. I look out at the forest, and I realize I'm the only human eyes to see this. I can feel the vastness of the planet and know that there is no other being that can fully understand me anywhere on it. I look back at the place where the wreckage of the colony is strewn over the field, and I can't help but cry for the friends I've lost, and the great hope of the colony, lost too.

I think back to my family, my sister and cousins. To them, I've been gone more than thirty years, even though it's only been a year for me. I wonder if they have forgotten me already. They don't even know I'm not on Earth anymore. My great-grandmother and grandparents are likely dead by now.

I'm learning my way, slowly, but everything is different. This planet is habitable, even comfortable, but so much is new and there is so much to learn in order to survive. Without the support of other people, everything seems harder. I can consult the encyclopedias and databases that I have access to, but all of the information about this planet we named Johannes is incomplete, and so much of it is just plain wrong.

And I have to keep hoping that I won't be alone forever. I'm eighteen now, and I won't see any more people until I'm 28. I can only assume that the third ship will find its way here after leaving Kepler 75f. There is so much work to do.

The Very Beginning: December 2102

As Trina walked through the narrow alley leading to the street, she looked up and saw only concrete and glass, then finally, dull grey sky. She missed the trees desperately. She missed seeing the leaves turn, missed hearing the breeze blow through them. She missed being able to feel the bark under her hands as she held on to branches, hefting her weight as high as she could go.

They'd lived in this neighborhood in the northern part of the Bronx for almost five years, after having been forced to move because their old neighborhood in Queens was flooded by the encroaching ocean. She liked the old neighborhood a lot better. She'd learned how to climb trees there, an activity she'd greatly enjoyed. Here, the only things to climb were fire escapes. It wasn't the same, but she liked climbing up high, and spending time looking down.

They lived in a big apartment complex full of tall, drab, gray buildings built in the '70s and '80s, as other parts of the city were increasingly underwater. They didn't really care how many people they could squeeze into the spaces left. She shared the small 2-bedroom apartment with her extended family of seven. In Queens, they'd shared a whole house. It wasn't big, but it was a lot roomier than what they had now.

She considered herself lucky, though. At age 6, she won a lottery spot to go to school, something her little sister hadn't. They both worked to support their family, but at least she didn't have to work as many hours as her sister did. And since her sister was so young, her work was only drudgery. At least Trina got to sit in a relatively quiet cubicle, while her sister was in a noisy factory.

As she walked down the street to her school Trina got lost in thought. She had been encouraged by her math teacher, who thought that Trina had promise. But they both were realistic—the chances that Trina would be able to win a scholarship to college was quite slim. More likely, she'd spend the rest of her life doing what she was doing now. But somewhere, deep inside, Trina knew her life would turn out differently. She didn't know why she knew, but she did.

As she approached the school, called "Bronxwood Preparatory Academy." Trina thought the name was antiquated, like the big thick columns in front. It was from another era, an era that didn't exist anymore. When there was something to actually prepare for. All but a tiny number of her fellow students would emerge from this school, prepared to do not much else except be a cog in the vast wheel that made other people rich. A wheel she was a part of and hated already.

Her first class of the day was physics, her favorite subject at the moment. She had stayed up until 3 a.m. this morning finishing her homework on fluid dynamics after she got home from work last night. As usual, she did all of the extra credit problem sets. They had been working on Pascal's law.

She walked into the classroom and sat in her seat, near the front. As her classmates entered, she watched equations appear on the front screen.

Her teacher, a light-skinned woman with tight black braids tied behind her head said, "Alright, people. Settle down.

"Today, we're going to make sure that you all fully understand Pascal's law. Can someone summarize for me what it is?"

Trina's hand shot up.

"Trina?"

"Pressure exerted on a liquid in a confined space is transmitted equally in all directions such that the pressure ratio stays the same."

"Good. Someone give me the equation."

George, who sat next to her, raised his hand.

"George?"

"Delta P equals p times g times delta h."

The equation went up on the board.

"Someone explain?"

Trina knew, but she waited a while before raising her hand.

"Trina?"

"Delta P is the hydrostatic pressure, p is the fluid density, g is gravity, delta h is the height of the fluid."

"Good."

The class went on, but Trina's mind wandered to one of the extra credit problem sets that she'd worked on last night. The question had been whether or not the Earth's atmosphere obeyed Pascal's law, and if not, how might one determine pressure depending upon where in the atmosphere one was. It had been a fun problem. Trina always enjoyed problems that involved things like that. She liked thinking big: things like how did the atmosphere work, and how might it be different if it was composed differently?

The rest of the day was a blur of mostly boring things. Her math teacher was out sick, and the substitute just handed out problems for all of them to solve. Problems she solved with lots of time to spare. She felt lucky to be in school, but she also felt frustrated by it. There was so much she wanted to learn, but she knew that she'd probably never get the chance.

She left school and walked to the subway to make her way to work. She climbed down the stairs, through the automatic payment aisle, then to the platform, and looked at the display. The next subway was due in 5 minutes. She leaned against the wall, thinking. It was almost time for Christmas, and her mother had already started to put out the decorations. Her mother loved Christmas. Trina always tried to get into the spirit to please her mom, and generally enjoyed the holiday, even though she didn't really feel it like her mother did. She hoped her mother wouldn't force her to go to church too much. It was the season her mom spent at church a lot.

The subway arrived, and Trina leaned against a pole on one side of the subway car. She looked at a very elderly lady, who occupied one of the two seats in the car. She was wearing an overcoat that looked too large for her. It was purple, and it looked like it had seen better days. The woman's hair was very thin and gray, and she coughed on occasion. Trina wondered what things had been like for her when she was Trina's age. The car wasn't too crowded this afternoon, which felt like a relief. It took about twenty minutes for the train to get from the station near school to Westchester, where she worked.

The company she worked for, CalSpace Tours, was the leading provider of space tours. She had applied for the job on a whim, not really expecting to get it. The job she had been working before was in Manhattan, where she worked in one of the fancy hotels, delivering room service meals. The competition for this job had been fierce, but she aced their tests, and aced her interview.

The company had some ships in orbit, and they did tours of the moon. She applied for the job simply because it had to do with space, but once she realized that she was going to spend all of her working hours selling space trips she dreamed of taking to people who could actually afford them, she started to hate it. It cost at least $250,000 for the most basic of trips to orbit for one day. Trips to the moon were more on the order of a million dollars. More than she could ever dream saving in her entire life. But after a while, it became rote, and her dreams of space slipped back into a pocket of her psyche, rarely to be looked at.

When she first came to the job, she was given a long list of leads, and she was supposed to contact each one through the voice network to try to sell them on the tours. It was completely disheartening at first. 60% of the people didn't respond in any way, and almost all of the rest just took her valuable time, but never actually signed up. Her first week was a complete disaster. She was sure she was going to be fired. She'd gone through less than ½ of her list in the time she was supposed to go through all of it.

But she found a system. She wondered about what would make people take a space trip. She dug up information about who had already signed up, ran the numbers, and then instead of contacting everyone on her list, she filtered it by the criteria that she'd discovered. Soon, she had a success rate that rivaled everyone's, and people wanted to know how she did it. She refused to tell them, because it was her security—she needed this job.

Today was a research day. She'd just gotten a new batch of leads, and she was researching them. She'd written a small program to get basic demographics for each person: age, marital status, gender, occupation and location, and filter the leads based on that data. Location told her how relatively wealthy they were. Age, marital status and gender told her about the likelihood that they might at all be interested.

Somewhat wealthy, middle-aged single or divorced men who worked in technical or engineering fields, and lived in California, Florida, Arizona and Texas, were by far the best candidates, and she always contacted them first. Anyone living in New England she didn't even bother with—if they wanted to go to space, they would do the contacting. Her next tier were very wealthy young couples that showed evidence of adventurousness—had they gone on eco-tours, or were they climbers or surfers?

After those, she cherry picked some based on instinct. She didn't know what it was about them that made her choose them, but she was almost always right. There were always some sorts of deals she could provide—extra time, or a cabin upgrade, or a discount. Trina knew which people would respond best to which deal.

By the end of her shift, she had a nice long list of likely folks she would contact tomorrow. It had been a good, productive day. And it was Friday. Her family would all be at home, making the weekly family dinner. That was one of the rituals of the family. Everyone was always home on Friday nights. Trina looked forward to it as she closed up her terminal and walked back to the subway home.

The next morning, Trina was fighting with the problem in front of her. It shouldn't be that hard, she was telling herself. She'd done plenty of problem sets like it before. This one was for extra, extra credit, but that didn't make it feel any less necessary to solve. The solution to the theorem had been eluding her for half an hour, and she was frustrated. She heard something and looked up to see her mother standing in the doorway, with a stern face.

"Trina!"

"Yes, Mom?"

"You are going to be late to work."

Trina looked at her display and swore under her breath. She'd been working on the problem for too long. She was going to be late to work. She was embarrassed and annoyed at the same time. She would much rather be struggling with this problem set than going to work.

"Sorry, Mom."

"Your sister will be home from work by six, and Nana will be home by seven, so we'll eat then."

As she got her things together, she said, "Mom, my shift doesn't end until midnight on Saturdays."

"Ah, right. Sorry. Well, we'll see you tomorrow morning then. Your father and I are going out dancing tonight after work for the first time in years. And remember, we're going to church tomorrow."

"That's great, mom. I hope you have fun." Trina was talking about both dancing and church, even though she knew her mother didn't interpret the statement that way. She was going to do what she could to get out of having to go to church with her parents. She hated it, and hated the stern, mean pastor, too.

She bolted out of their apartment, giving her mother a quick kiss on the way out. Walking down the dark, narrow hallway, she tried to avoid the garbage strewn around, but it was dim—the hall was only lit by a single coiled bulb that flickered. The tiny elevator always stank of urine and vomit; she tried to hold her breath until she got onto the ground floor. She wove her way through the labyrinthine halls to the outside, then to the subway.

As she arrived at the station where her work was, Trina realized that she hadn't made up any time during the trip, so she bolted from the station, and ran to her building. She was going to be about ten minutes late. At the building door, she put her face in front of the retina identification system, and heard the door click. She entered, went up the stairs, and down the hall to where her cubicle was. She sat down and turned on her system.

"You're late again, Ms. Dewing." Trina looked up to see her manager looking down at her with a sour face.

"Sorry Mr. Wilkins. I was…"

"I don't want to hear an excuse. Late again, and you're gone, you hear me?"

She nodded. Of course, she knew his threat was empty. He'd given that threat a half-dozen times before. She was by far the most productive member of his crew. It would be crazy for him to fire her, no matter how often she was late. But she tried not to tempt fate.

It was a long day, but given her research yesterday, she did well, booking quite a number of people onto space tours. One particular conversation stood out.

"Hello, I'm looking for Mr. Quirin Nilsson," Trina said in her most perky sales voice. Mr. Nilsson was an especially good lead, as he was divorced, 50-something, lived in Texas, and was a very well-paid executive in a large tech corporation. There was data that he'd been in space before, care of Solar Exploratory. And he was not at all risk-averse, as he had interests like sky diving and rock climbing. He was a prime candidate for a Moon trip.

"Yes, this is he."

"This is CalSpace Tours calling. Do you know us?"

He grunted, said, "Yes," and nothing more.

"Mr. Nilsson, we are running a special on our trips to the Moon. I've seen you've gone into orbit before."

"Yes." Silence.

"Would you like to hear about our special?"

"No, not really. May I ask you a question?"

"Of course, sir."

"Would you take a trip like this?"

"Well, sir, honestly, I couldn't possibly…"

"I mean, if money were no object."

"Well, then, yes, sir, I would. No question about it. I've always wanted to go into space."

"Always?"

"Since I was a child, and first learned that there were places people could go out there. When I learned about the moon, and that people had visited it, and about the other planets and the stars. I've always…" Trina caught herself.

"I'm so sorry, sir."

"No reason to apologize. What's your name?"

"Trina Dewing." There was a pause.

"From Brooklyn?"

"Ah, yes sir."

"Just so you know, I am an investor in Solar Exploratory."

"And…"

"That means that I won't take a CalSpace tour. I'm going out to the asteroid belt in a few weeks." Trina was instantly jealous but didn't let on. "Well, sir, I'm sorry to have taken your time. I do hope that you have a good trip."

"Thank you, Ms. Dewing. And if you ever think about a job with Solar Exploratory, I've flagged your name in our database."

"Thank you, sir, but I doubt…"

"You never know. Keep optimistic, Ms. Dewing."

Trina smiled. He seemed like a really nice man.

"Thank you, sir. Have a nice night."

She took a break to get something to eat, then started her last set of calls to California. She managed to book another few people for the Moon trip, and a couple for a trip into orbit. She looked at the clock. It was 11:47. Her shift ended at midnight. She was almost done. She flagged some people she would contact tomorrow evening, during her next shift. Sundays were good to contact certain people, and not others. Her work night finally ended, and she made her way home.

As she left the elevator on her floor in the apartment building and walked toward her apartment, she heard a commotion. She turned the corner to see people spilling out of the door.

"Ah, Trina!" Her grandmother approached her, tears in her eyes.

"What's happening, Nana? It's so late."

"Come inside, child."

She walked in to see a lot of relatives she hadn't seen since her cousin's wedding a couple of years ago. She realized that this must mean that someone died. Maybe her great-grandmother? She looked around for her parents but didn't see them. Everyone was surrounding her all of a sudden.

"What's going on?" she said.

Her Nana said, "Trina, your parents were killed in an accident."

"What?" She couldn't get her mind around that. She'd just seen her mother that afternoon.

"The floor of the dance hall collapsed. They were killed along with twenty other people."

Trina remembered that tonight was the night they were going dancing. Her mother had been looking forward to it for weeks. It was horrible to think that her parents died that way. Trina was paralyzed. How was she going to take care of her sister? How could they possibly afford to keep this apartment? She didn't know what she was going to do.

The rest of the night was a blur. She cried, a lot, and was eventually helped to her bed. She slept. When she woke up, at first, she was sure it was a dream. But then she saw her cousin Bettina sleeping on the floor near her bed. She looked over to see her little sister looking at her, sad eyes full of tears. She got up, and then sat on her sister's bed.

"It will be alright, Mita. I'll take care of you. I promise."

Mita was crying, and Trina held her for a while. After a time, there was a knock on the door.

"Trina?"

"Yes, Nana."

"Will you get dressed and come out here, please?"

"OK."

Trina got dressed, and washed up, and went out into the living room, where her grandfather Clevon and Nana, and great-grandmother LeShawna, and her uncle and aunt were sitting.

She sat down.

Her uncle said, "Trina, your parents left a lot of debt."

Trina was silent. She didn't know what to say. She knew this was the truth. Her mother's parents had died deeply in debt, some of those debts had been from their parents, and her family had been working hard to survive, and pay it off.

"The family is responsible to pay it."

Trina said, "I'm working, I can help. If it means I need to quit school, I will, so I can work two or three jobs."

"That's not enough, Trina."

"What do you mean?"

Her uncle sighed. "Because the debt is three generations old now, they are demanding immediate payment of all of it."

"But how can we pay it?"

"We only have one choice. We have to sell the labor contract of either you or your sister."

Trina had heard about this but hadn't really thought much about it before now. She remembered from a history lesson at school about a time in the past when debt could be forgiven, and it was not passed on from parent to child at death. But for as long as Trina had been alive, the debts of the parents became the debts of the children, and her family was still working to pay the debts of her great-grandparents. The one way you could possibly pay your debts in full was to sell your labor contract if you were young enough.

She vaguely remembered a few years ago when her father was almost thirty-five, the cut-off age. He and her mother argued about it for a while, but they decided that he would keep working, instead of selling his contract.

She knew that once you sold your labor contract, you worked without hope of freedom, or seeing family, or anything for life. It didn't sound like a good life, but she knew that if she did this, it would free her family from her parent's debt. That would mean that they could afford to bury her parents, stay in the apartment, and maybe her sister would have some chance for a decent life. It was worth it.

"Alright. I'll do it."

Her Nana started to cry. "I hate to lose you and my children at the same time!" She sobbed and was comforted by her husband. Trina was simply numb. She got up to get herself something to eat. Somewhere in her head, she heard, "What a great Christmas present this is."

Two days later, after most of the extended family had left, a man came to the door. Trina was in the living room, talking with her cousin Bettina. She watched her grandfather answer it.

"I'm here to pick up Trina Dewing."

Trina looked up, then got up and walked towards him.

"I'm Trina. Give me a moment to gather…"

He said in a toneless voice, "You will need nothing. It will all be taken from you anyway, so there is no point in gathering anything."

She nodded.

"Trina, hold out your arm, please."

She did, and he took out a long, slim cylinder with a handle with a somewhat larger diameter and placed the end against her upper arm. He pushed a button, and she felt a very sharp pain in her arm. Even after he removed the cylinder, it still stung.

He said, "It's a geo-location device. We can find you no matter what."

"I wasn't planning on going anywhere."

"Some people want to escape, you see."

She nodded.

He took out a phone and did something on it. He looked at her grandfather.

"Your family's debt is now provisionally paid. You may receive a small bonus depending upon Trina's behavior and test scores in a few weeks."

Her grandfather said, "Thank you."

"Time to go," the man said sharply.

She was hugged by everyone, and as she walked out of the apartment, she turned back to see a wall of tearful family, and her sister sobbing. She followed the man feeling nothing. They left her apartment block, and got into a car, which then started moving through the traffic.

He didn't say anything to her, so she just looked out of the windows, watching people and places they were going through. Trina could tell they were headed north. Eventually, the car entered a large highway, one that Trina had never seen before, and started to go very quickly. Everything became a blur.

Trina lay her head back on the seat and closed her eyes. She thought she was cried out, but the tears for her family, and her life, came anyway. She had no idea what was coming next, and she missed her parents terribly already, but she was at least glad that she'd given her family a chance to move on, and her sister a chance for a decent life. She hated to think she'd never see them again.

The car slowed, and then stopped, and the door next to her opened. She got out, and the door closed behind her. She looked forward and saw a number of people getting out of vehicles, and going toward a building, so she followed.

Once she entered the building, she could hear a voice drone, "Please pass through the archway. A color will flash on the screen in front of you. Follow the line on the floor with your color." The voice repeated the message, over and over. A line was forming in front of the arch, and Trina entered it.

The building was nondescript: the inside was the same as pretty much any commercial building she'd been in. She looked around at the variety of people—people she imagined were in the same predicament as she was. There weren't very many her age, most seemed in their early 30s. There were plenty of women and men. Everyone looked either bored or scared. She was one of the scared ones.

She stopped briefly below the arch, and the color blue was flashed on the display. She found the blue line in the floor and followed it down a long hallway. She entered a waiting room, where about ten other people her age were sitting. She found a chair and sat down to wait.

Every ten minutes or so, someone's name would be called, and they would go through a door. An image of her mother that last morning telling her she would be late to work came unbidden to her mind, and she cried again, hiding her face in her hands.

"Trina Dewing."

She wiped her face on her sleeves, and got up, and went through the door that was now open. She walked down another hall and saw a blue light above one of the doors—it was open, and she walked through. She saw a plain-looking woman with dark hair and dark eyes in a white uniform sitting in front of a desk.

"Come in and sit down." Trina heard the door click behind her. She sat down.

The woman said in a bored tone, "The terms of your indenture are as follows: You are the property of Labor Systems International until your tenure is finished. Your family's debt has been provisionally removed, and interest on the debt will no longer accrue. However, should you do anything which, in our judgment, decreases the value of your labor, we reserve the right to consider this agreement null and void, and your family will still be responsible for the rest of the debt. In your particular family's case, this means that your younger sister will be required to sell her labor contract."

"What could I do to decrease the value of my labor?"

The woman looked annoyed, "I'm getting to that."

"OK, sorry."

She continued, "Things that Labor Systems International considers to endanger the value of your labor includes use of alcohol, tobacco, cannabis or any other drugs except expressly prescribed for you by one of our doctors, eating anything except the diet we provide you, engaging in any sexual activity with members of the opposite sex, assaulting or threatening anyone, sleeping for less or more than your prescribed time period, questioning the orders of your superiors, trying to escape from service, or trying to end your life."

"And I have to follow that for how long?"

"The longer you follow the rules, the less the debt is."

"How long?"

She looked down, then back up. "Your family's debt is quite large. Your tenure is forty-five years."

"What happens after that?"

"You are released."

Trina didn't believe it. She'd never heard or seen anyone who'd been released from this. Besides, she'd be really old then. But she didn't say anything.

"You will be given a battery of tests, physical, mental and psychological, and Labor Systems International retains the right to assign you to any work duty that it deems appropriate or sell your contract to any eligible bidder. Do you understand all of this?"

She nodded.

"I need you to sign this, please. It basically states what I just said. She pushed a tablet toward Trina, with a stylus. Trina decided to read what it was anyway. There was some other language around the debt and her family in case she did not fulfill her tenure, but she didn't bother to read all of it. She'd fulfill the tenure, she was sure. She signed it.

The woman asked, "Any questions?"

Trina had a million, but she'd find the answer to all of them eventually. She shook her head.

"Alright. Go, and keep following the blue line."

Trina got up, left the room, and followed the line. She ended up in another waiting room, with a variety of people. Everyone here looked to be younger than 20.

"Hi, my name is Manuela." She looked to her right to see a young woman with a plump face and dark eyes and long, straight hair holding out her hand. Trina shook it.

"I'm Trina."

"Where did you live?"

"The Bronx. 222nd and Bronxwood."

"I came from the Bronx, too. Not that far from you. Did your parents give you up? Mine did."

Trina couldn't imagine parents selling their child's contract. They must have been desperate. "No, my parents died a few days ago in an accident. The only way my family could bury them and afford to move on was for me to do this."

"I'm so sorry, that sounds horrible."

Trina nodded. "But there wasn't much to do. I imagine the same was true for your parents."

Manuela shook her head and looked sad. "My father could have done this—it was his gambling debts that got them into the mess. But he refused. My mother didn't have a choice. I have a younger sister and brother. She couldn't sell her contract, because she knew my father wouldn't take care of us. So, I had to."

"Wow, that sounds terrible. I'm sorry."

"It's alright. At least I know they will be fine. And my tenure is only fifteen years."

Trina almost asked whether she'd ever heard of anyone who was released, but she decided that it wasn't a good idea.

"My tenure is forty-five years."

"Oh my! I'm so sorry. That's a long time."

Trina nodded. They talked for a while about school. Manuela had also won the school lottery and was in the only arts school left in the city.

"They said I had real talent at dancing. I hope I am assigned to something that allows me to dance."

"I do too."

They heard a voice speak, "Transport to testing facility leaving in three minutes."

Manuela said, "I wonder what the testing is like?"

"I guess we'll find out, won't we?"

After a while, double doors opened, and a light flashed above the door. "Transport to testing facility now boarding."

They all got up, and went through the doors, and saw a bus sitting with its door open. They filed in, and Manuela and Trina sat together toward the back.

"I still can't believe we're not supposed to have sex. That sounds just so… awful. Not to have sex for fifteen years. And you! You can't have sex for forty-five!"

Trina decided this was not the time to tell Manuela that she had no interest in the opposite sex. She just nodded but said nothing. Manuela was talkative, which felt helpful to Trina. The last thing she wanted to do was think about what was happening, and Manuela seemed to only require the occasional "Uh huh" and "Yes" and "Really?" It managed to fill the time, until Manuela eventually stopped talking.

Trina looked out of the bus windows and let the landscape drift by her. At one point, the bus slowed, and she could see her parents sitting by the side of the road, waving to her. She got up to ask the driver to stop, but there was no driver, and she turned around, and there was no one else on the bus anymore. She watched out of the windows as her parents got further and further behind them.

"We're here!" Trina heard, and was startled awake, to see Manuela looking at her strangely.

"Are you OK?" She asked.

"Sorry, fine. I just fell asleep." Trina didn't bother to tell Manuela about the deep sadness the dream had left her with. They'd been on the bus for what must have been hours. Trina hadn't eaten since breakfast, and her stomach was grumbling.

They arrived, somewhere, and got out and went toward another nondescript looking commercial building. Before she entered the building, she looked at the surroundings. They definitely were nowhere near where she had lived. There were a lot of trees in the distance, and it was flat and open.

As they walked in, Trina could see large photographs of people doing varied things. There seemed to be nurses, and farmers, and a lot of other vocations.

Manuela tugged her sleeve. "See that dancer? Maybe I can be a dancer!"

A voice said, "Make your way to the cafeteria, on your left," and repeated over and over again. They followed, and entered into this very large cafeteria, where there were many people—far more than Trina had seen so far. They got in line, and got a tray with a prepackaged, preheated meal. They sat across from each other on the end of a long table.

"This looks disgusting," Manuela said.

"Yeah." Trina opened the packaging. There was brown rice, a big pile of some kind of green vegetable, and a slab of some unidentifiable material. It was definitely not meat. It didn't taste so bad, however, and Trina was hungry.

"Dining period is now over. Proceed to your assigned rooms. If you have just arrived, make your way out of the door with the green light."

They got up, put their trays in the bin where everyone was placing them, and walked through the door with the green light.

The Labor Contract: December 2102

Trina woke and couldn't figure out where she was. Then she remembered and sighed. The day before had been confusing, and she still couldn't get her bearings. After dinner, they had been given a small bag with two uniforms, slippers and toiletries. She had to remove all of her jewelry, and she was told to discard the clothes she came with. They were ushered into this strange shower, which seemed to somehow, with just water and soap, to scrub her until she was raw. Then, they shaved her head. She watched the dreadlocks she had so carefully cultivated since she was 12 drop to the floor.

She shared a room with eleven other women, in tri-level bunk beds. She had been so tired that she'd gone right to sleep, but she'd awakened a few times during the night, after having had nightmares. She was on the top bunk. She didn't know what time it was, but she couldn't stay lying down anymore.

Once she was down and was padding in her bare feet toward the bathroom, a sharp screeching sound started, and then a voice said, "It is time to get up. You have ten minutes before you are due to the cafeteria for breakfast."

She guessed she had good timing. She brushed her teeth with the new toothbrush and toothpaste they had provided, washed her face, and then walked toward the cafeteria.

Breakfast was oatmeal, with some dried fruit, and milk. There was also a small glass of some sort of orange flavored drink. Manuela found her and sat across from her.

"Trina, are you OK? I heard you crying last night."

"Yeah, I'm OK. I just miss my parents."

"I understand." Manuela was silent for once. Trina wondered what she was thinking.

"All new arrivals, go to room 45 for initial testing. Second day individuals go to room 101 for testing. Third day individuals go to room 215 for testing. Fourth day individuals go to room 325 for final assignments."

Trina said, "OK, three days of testing, then you get an assignment. Maybe we won't be bored."

"I was talking to a cute guy who was doing his third day. He said the testing was completely baffling, with all sorts of questions that couldn't be answered. He hated it."

"You could have not told me that."

Manuela laughed. "I'm sorry."

"It's alright. Whatever. We have to go through it anyway."

They got up, followed the people they knew arrived with them last night. There were signs in the halls, so it was easy to find room 45. It was a large room, with many cubicles. Sort of like where she worked. They heard, "Find a seat."

Trina heard screaming at one end of the room. Two people seemed to be fighting over the same cubicle. It was strange to Trina, since there were more than enough, and they all looked completely the same. Two burly-looking men rushed in, and grabbed both of the women who were arguing, and took them out of the room.

A voice different than the ever-present instructive voice said, "Note: behavior like that will make your agreement null and void. We have a zero-tolerance policy toward violent behavior."

Trina thought, *note to self: avoid conflict at all cost.*

She sat at a cubicle, and the screen in front of her said "Press here to start." She did.

There were a long series of multiple-choice questions. They started out extremely easy. They ranged from science and math, to history, technology, and even current events. They got a break for lunch, and then the questions continued for the rest of the afternoon. They did get slightly more difficult as the day wore on, but even those questions were easy for Trina to answer.

At dinner, Trina asked Manuela how it had gone for her. Manuela said, "It was OK at first, but after lunch it was very hard. The last hour or two I was sure I didn't get anything right. What about you?"

Trina lied. "About the same." She wasn't sure why she lied—maybe she didn't want Manuela to feel bad.

The next day, the routine was the same, except this time, they went to room 101. It had the same cubicles, and the same screens. But the questions were very different. First, there were multiple choice questions about feelings. Then, there were stories, and they were supposed to write how they would deal with the situations in the stories. Trina felt like she had no idea how she was doing, or what they were looking for, but she did the best she could. The third day was quite different. When they arrived in room 215, there were no cubicles, but there were poles coming down from the ceiling, and screens attached at the bottom, around eye level for most people. Trina stood in front of one and pushed the screen.

"Do the following exercise as many times as you can before you get out of breath. The screen then showed a woman doing jumping jacks. Trina obeyed, and she could see the people around her doing jumping jacks as well. There were sit ups, and pushups, and other kinds of tests. Some in the room couldn't do much. Trina was in the middle. She hadn't had much exercise since they moved from Brooklyn. Before, there were places she could run, and roam, and climb trees. In the Bronx, everywhere was crowded and dangerous. She couldn't really go far.

At lunch, as had happened each day before, a few names were called. Today, hers was one. Not knowing that Trina would never see her again, she bid Manuela a brief goodbye, and went to room 234. The door was open, and she walked in expecting more tests, but a man was sitting at a desk. He was the first person she'd seen who wasn't being tested, besides the two burly security men the first day.

"Hello, Trina, sit down, please."

She sat.

"You'll be happy to know that you are one of a few people who are eligible to have your services sold to another vendor."

"What does that mean?"

"It means that you have tested above the 95th percentile on one of your tests. In fact, you've tested at the 99th percentile in your age group in the intelligence and knowledge test, and in the 96th percentile in the psychological test."

"So, what's next?"

"You'll stay here for a few more days. We have to give you many more tests, to find out who might want to bid on your services. If the bid is high, your family will benefit. And once your contract is sold, your family's debt is permanently wiped out."

"That sounds like a good thing."

"Yes, it is a good thing. Please go to your room and get your bag, and go section five, room 502."

"OK."

Trina left and went back to the empty room. She grabbed her bag and went to section five. She found room 502 and walked in. A tall, blond woman greeted her.

"Hi Trina. I'll take the bag for now. You'll be sleeping and eating in room 530. Please go sit in one of those cubicles over there." She pointed to the corner of the room.

The questions Trina was faced with this time were far more complex than the ones she was given earlier. There were problem sets to solve, programs to create, and essays to write. By the time the test was over, she was exhausted. But she also knew that she'd done well with most of the things she'd been given.

The next four days went by in a blur. There were a lot more tests, there was a three-hour conversation she had with someone about her family and how she felt about losing her parents. They even asked her what her dreams were. She surprised herself by telling them that she spent a lot of time working for a company that sold trips to space, and that she had always wanted to go into space. It was true, but she had buried that dream for so long, that it seemed a surprise to her that it came out.

Finally, it seemed she was done. She was left in the small room that she'd been living in—it had a bed, a table where she took her meals, and an attached bathroom. It felt luxurious to her—she'd never had a whole room and bathroom to herself.

She took a nap, and was awakened by a voice "Trina Dewing, report to room 501." She got up and went out to find the room. She went in and was greeted by the same blond woman she'd been seeing each day for the last four days.

"Trina, I have some very good news for you."

"Yes?"

"Your labor contract has been sold to Kepler Exploratory."

Trina had never heard of them.

"What will I be doing?"

"I don't know. I'm sorry."

"Who are they?"

"I don't know that, either."

Trina didn't quite know what to say.

"They'll be picking you up momentarily."

"So, my family's debt is paid permanently?"

"Oh, yes. They even received a bonus."

Trina smiled. At least something good is coming of this.

The blond looked pensive for a moment, then said, "They are here. Come with me."

"Should I get…"

"No, they will provide you with everything you need." Somehow, losing the little she had yet again was jarring, but she didn't seem to have a choice in the matter.

She followed the woman through some corridors, and through a series of heavy security doors, to the outside. There was a man standing next to a small car, quite informally dressed in jeans and a t-shirt that said, "To the moon, Alice." Trina didn't get the reference. They walked toward him.

The woman said to the man, "Here's Trina Dewing. I take it everything went through fine."

He said, "It did, yes."

"Good. Tell Richard it was a pleasure doing business with you folks."

"Will do."

Trina could tell there was something in his voice that seemed strained somehow. She watched the blond walk away.

"Trina, hi there. My name is Joel." He actually had his hand out for her to shake it. It seemed weird, but she shook it.

"I know this is all very strange, but believe me, this is your lucky day. Here, get in. We have a short drive to the airport, then we're flying to Nevada."

"Nevada?"

"Yup. Middle of nowhere Nevada. That's where the training and launch facility is."

"Launch?"

"They didn't tell you?"

"Er, no, she didn't know."

He snorted. "I can never figure those people out. She knows."

He got in on the other side of the car.

He said, "Akron Fulton International Airport, please."

A voice spoke from the car dash, "Acknowledged."

"Well, why don't I give you the short picture while we're on our way, eh?"

Trina nodded.

"Kepler Exploratory is a space exploratory company. We have several public projects, such as the missions to Mars and the asteroid belt—you've heard about those?"

"Yes, I've been following them for a while, but I don't remember the name Kepler Exploratory."

"Those are done by a subsidiary, Solar Exploratory."

"Solar Exploratory—right, I've heard of them."

"Good. There is the big project that is not public, and that's what we've recruited you for."

"And that is?"

"We're sending ships to three planets of relatively close stars that we think might be habitable."

Trina was awestruck. "What?"

He looked at her and smiled.

"Yes, we're going into space, to a different star."

Trina could hardly believe her ears. And she couldn't figure out how this happened.

"I don't get it. Aren't there thousands of people trying to get on missions like this?"

He smiled again. "There would be if they were public. The investors want these missions to be completely secret, which means recruiting for them is nearly impossible. They don't even want applicants to know where they are going or what they are doing—and as you can imagine, most applicants don't like that sort of thing. We mostly get folks who have proved themselves on the other missions. We've taken on a few from LSI, but didn't plan on taking any more, but your name was flagged for some reason, so here you are."

"I know why."

"You do?"

"Just before my parents were killed, I was trying to sell a space tour to this guy who turned out to be an investor of Solar Exploratory. We had a nice conversation, and he told me he'd flag my name in the database, but I never thought…"

Joel smiled, "I guess it made a difference."

Trina smiled. "Yeah. Wow. I'm really going into space?"

"That you are."

"I need some time to get my head around this. One minute I was indentured for forty-five years, the next minute…"

"Once you go, though, you aren't ever coming home, you know."

"That's alright. I didn't expect to ever get home anyway."

"True that—you'd never get home."

"How much do you know about LSI?"

He said, "A lot. More than most people."

"Is it really true that they release people after their tenure is up? I'd never met or heard of anyone in my life who had gone back home after selling their labor contract."

"Those are convenient lies they tell, one that you are actually going to be indentured to them, for some specified term, and that you'll get to be released after. They sell the contracts of every single person, mostly to China and Southeast Asia, and southern and eastern Africa. People work in farms and factories over there and die there. They never come back. LSI sells their contracts for two or three times what their family's debt was. The testing is to weed out those who will be completely useless and find the few at the top they can sell for really top dollar, like you."

Trina thought back to Manuela, who, upon seeing a dancer in that picture gallery of things that people might end up doing, seemed hopeful of the future. She was sad to think of Manuela ending up in China or someplace doing factory work or farming. She sighed.

Trina shook her head and said, "Enough of that. What's next?"

Joel smiled again. Trina was beginning to like him.

"Well, there's a rigorous physical training program—that's one of the most important things. If you go don't into cryosleep at your physical peak, you'll leave cryosleep in a state that won't be useful for too long. We want you useful within a few days of waking."

"I've heard of the concept of cryosleep, but I didn't know it had been used."

"It's new. We've done a lot of testing, and we're pretty confident of it, but it's harsh. Unfortunately, we'll get to experience it firsthand. There will be orientation, getting to know equipment and such. We launch in 6 months. You're one of the last recruits."

"So, you're coming too?"

"Yup. I'm your supervisor."

"What will I be doing? Can I be a pilot?"

He laughed. "I hate to tell you—you might be very smart, and emotionally and psychologically stable to boot, but you have no training. You're going to be a basic grunt. Sorry."

"It's OK, I guess that's what I should have expected."

"When we land at the colony, and work starts in earnest there, you'll be on the same footing as every other grunt and get a chance to make something of yourself. That's why today is your lucky day."

They arrived at the airport and made their way to a small jet that was sitting on the tarmac. Trina had never been in a plane before. Once they got in, the pilot came to close the doors—they were the only passengers. It was dark when they took off, so the only thing Trina could see out of the windows were lights down below.

It was strange in a way. Flying was something that none of her family had ever done—it was a luxury beyond them. She wished she could describe it for her sister, who would appreciate the adventure of it. It was a surprisingly short trip for the distance Trina knew they were traveling. When they landed, she followed Joel, and they got into a little cart, which he drove to a large, squat building that was not so far from where the plane landed.

Joel said, "Home sweet home." He parked the cart among a few others.

"Follow me."

They walked into the building, which Trina could see was full of varied sorts of equipment and supplies. It was as chaotic and cluttered as the LSI buildings were spare and boring.

A slight brunette walked up to them. "Joel, you're back. And I see you brought Trina."

"Indeed, I did. Trina, meet Ryenne Vickery. She's my boss, and operations manager for all of these missions."

Ryenne had her hand out, and Trina shook it. "Welcome Trina. I know this feels weird to you. You'll get used to it. We treat everyone the same here. I'm assuming you won't try to escape." She smiled.

Trina said, "Are you kidding? And miss a chance to be in space? No way!" They all laughed.

"Come to my office, Trina, there are a few things we need to go over. Then I'll show you round and get you what you need. That uniform they gave you is… well… we need to get you some real clothes."

She followed Trina back to her office, which was even more cluttered, if possible, with equipment and paper. Ryenne cleaned off a chair.

"Please, sit."

Trina sat.

"I expect Joel gave you a bit of a review of the situation?"

"He did. We're going to a habitable planet of a nearby star to colonize it."

"Yes, you are."

"And I'm going to be a grunt."

Ryenne laughed. "Well, yes. Your official title will be 'Colony Associate.' Translates to 'grunt'. You will basically do whatever Joel tells you to do. He's a good guy, he won't abuse his authority."

Trina nodded. "I got that impression."

"And I imagine he told you that once things get going on the colony, you'll have a chance like everyone else to make something of yourself."

"He did."

"Great. There are a couple of things to tell you. All of the other people on this mission were recruited from Solar Exploratory and aren't indentured. They are being paid, although since we're never coming back, most of that pay is going to their families. You, however, won't be getting paid."

"I assumed that."

"Once you're in the colony, and you've got some systems in place, you will be like everyone else, and eligible for paid employment, whatever that will mean in the colony. But not now."

Trina nodded. "Look, Joel said that today was my lucky day, and I know he was right. Just getting the chance to get into space, and explore somewhere new, is totally worth it all."

Ryenne smiled. "The other thing is that we cannot let you contact your family. First, it is against the contract we signed with LSI, and this mission is secret. I'm sorry about that."

"It's alright. I didn't expect to be able to contact them anyway, and they need to just let me go."

Ryenne looked grim, but then her face softened. "Look, let's get you some clothes, and a place to lay your head. The cafeteria is in the building next door. Are you hungry?"

"Yeah, I haven't eaten since breakfast."

"OK, let's get you some food."

Trina had to admit that she was enjoying herself. The food in the cafeteria was good, the clothes she was given were comfortable and functional, and she shared a room with only three other women, all of whom seemed really nice. In six months, she'd be on a spaceship to some unknown place. She smiled. She would much rather still have her parents, but if she couldn't, she certainly could not have imagined a better result.

Journal Entry, January 23, 2103

I've been in Nevada for more than three weeks, now. I'm getting used to the new reality, but every time I wake up in the morning, I'm still confused. And every night I still dream of my parents, my family, and home. The dreams are so vivid and real.

Everyone is being nice to me, and I'm enjoying the work. We have several hours of physical training each day, mostly so that the twenty years we spend in cryosleep won't completely make us useless. We also have lots of briefings, and meetings to talk about colony logistics.

Everyone is excited about the prospect of exploration of new systems. There is a big undercurrent of urgency I don't quite understand, and no one has explained to me yet. It's not just about meeting the schedule so that we can launch on time—we are in great shape, and there is not much danger of that. It's something else. Hopefully soon, I'll figure it out, or someone will give me a clue.

For being just a grunt, I feel like they've given me a lot of responsibility, which makes me nervous. Already, Joel has put me in charge of making sure that we will have the building materials we'll need for the colony on board the *Precious Hope*. It has meant I've had to learn about weight restrictions and requirements, building materials, and a lot of logistical details on how things get from Earth up to the ship, which was built in orbit.

Joel and Ryenne seem to think that I'm smart and responsible, and although I think of myself that way, mostly, it still feels strange, to be treated like an adult. And I worry constantly about whether I'm really measuring up to their expectations. I hope I do.

I think about Mita and the rest of the family a lot. I dream about them, too. I know that they've buried mom and dad by now and must be getting on in their life. I hope that Mita was able to use my school spot, and maybe she'll be able to go to school for at least a few years. I miss them terribly.

And I can't help but wonder where Manuela is, and how she is. I imagine her on some field, picking a crop, or in some factory, and I feel bad for her. I can't imagine living a life like that. And I can't help but think about how lucky I was to avoid that life.

Preparations for Launch: March 2103

"Go, go, go!" Trina was climbing the wall as fast as she could. She had last done the wall in three minutes, and her personal goal was to get up the wall in two. Most people took about four minutes to climb the wall, but she wanted to do better than that.

She got up in two minutes and forty-five seconds. That was better than last time. She climbed down more slowly, and dropped to the ground, catching her breath. She felt a hand on her shoulder. It was Joel.

"You are a champion climber. You're the best of the bunch, now."

"I love to climb."

"You know there's a taller wall."

"Where?"

"I'll take you there tomorrow. You'll love it."

The next day, she, Joel, and several of her colleagues were in a small van, driving somewhere. She didn't have any idea where they were going, and at the moment, she didn't care. She liked the training, and she could tell she was getting stronger. The orientation had been fascinating, and Joel had given her some particularly interesting assignments, which she enjoyed doing. It had been three months since she arrived, and the place already felt like home, and the people felt like family. She'd gotten to know two people in particular; both were on this trip with her to the "bigger wall."

Cayenne was a Native American from South Dakota. She'd been recruited by Solar Exploratory and had been working in the asteroid belt until they asked her to join this crew. She was at least fifteen years older than Trina and had become a sort of big sister to her. And then there was Henry, who was just a little older than she was, from Texas. Apparently, his father was a friend of one of the investors, and thought that this would be good for Henry, who hadn't quite found his way.

They enjoyed talking with one another—he came from such a different background than she did, and they both were curious about each other's lives and situations.

Henry said, "I bet he's taking us to a cliff."

Trina said, "A cliff? Like a real cliff? Wow. That will be fun. I've never seen a cliff in real life."

"Well, it's more dangerous than an indoor climbing wall. And there's all sorts of stuff to learn about how to climb it."

"Yeah, but isn't that all part of the fun?"

Henry laughed. Trina could see some hills arising in the distance—hills you couldn't see from the compound out in the middle of the desert. They eventually went off of the paved road, onto a rough dirt road. They stopped in the shadow of a very tall cliff.

Joel said, "Alright, out of the van, everyone. Let's teach you all how to climb a real wall."

Trina was excited she loved climbing, and being high up, able to see so much from that vantage point.

Cayenne stood next to Trina, looking up. She said, "Oh, boy. This isn't quite my thing."

Henry said, "It'll be fun, Cayenne, really."

Cayenne just shook her head, but she was smiling.

Joel said, "Folks, gather round. We'll be climbing this cliff, using technical climbing techniques. It could be free-climbed, but you all are far too valuable for me to risk that, so we'll be using ropes today."

Joel spent time explaining the use of the ropes, and pitons, carabineers, and other equipment. They climbed an easy part of the cliff, then Joel, Henry, Trina, and a man named Hakim, who was always very quiet, decided to climb to the top together. Trina loved it and wished she would have had a chance to do more of it before she left Earth, but she knew that was unlikely.

At the top, Trina asked Joel, "Do you think there are cliffs like this on Kepler 75f?"

Joel said, "No idea, Trina. We haven't gotten back all the data yet from the probe we sent back in 2090. In fact, we won't get that data until we're on route."

"Well, I hope there are. I would love to get to climb more."

Joel said, "God, I'm glad we got you, Trina. You would have been so wasted in a Chinese factory."

They rappelled down the cliff, then got back into the van, and ate sandwiches on the way back to the compound.

Joel said, "Crew, tomorrow's a big day. We finally get the full mission briefing. You'll love it."

So far, Trina and the rest of the crew had only really gotten little snippets of what would happen. She knew that she'd be in cryosleep, and that she'd be working to build the colony, and she'd gleaned some details from the work assignments, but the pieces weren't connected yet. It would be good to get the full picture of what was in store for them.

The next day, she was fidgeting in her seat, waiting for the briefing to begin. The entire crew of 110 were sitting together in the auditorium of the compound. It was the first time she'd seen everyone. She'd gotten to know most of the people in her section, which was "Colony Logistics," but she hadn't met many in and of the other sections, which included "Science," "Flight Engineering," and "Agronomy," plus a lot of others.

A tall, well-built, tanned man, with straight, jet-black hair that had patches of gray at the temples, walked up to the front. He spoke with a slight accent.

"Hello, I am Captain Duval Chenè. I'm the captain of the *Precious Hope*, the ship that will take us to Kepler 75f." There was applause, and Trina couldn't help but join in.

"Thank you. Let's get this started, shall we? I send greetings from the investors of Kepler Exploratory. They have great optimism about the crew that we have gathered, and they are very much looking forward to the success of this mission.

"First, I want to address the 'why' of this mission. For many of you, just the idea of exploring a new star system, and starting human life somewhere new, is enough of a draw. Like you, I am one of those. For me, this is the adventure of a lifetime, and to take part in this new phase of human history is enough.

"But many people, including the investors, are deeply worried about the continued viability of life on Earth. And they see this as an essential mission to help prevent our extinction as a species. You don't have to hold that view, but I do want you to understand what many see as an important backdrop. If things continue as they have on Earth, those of us who will have settled other stars might well be what's left of humanity.

"We are going to one of the three systems that the investors of Kepler Exploratory have chosen. The *Precious Hope* is one of nine ships that will be sent. Three have already left, the first one for Kepler 75f, the second for Kepler 65g, and one just left for Kepler 57d a year ago. Eventually, the last ship to leave will also head to Kepler 75f, joining us ten years after we arrive."

The captain introduced a scientist, who explained why the three systems were chosen. It made sense to Trina. They were three of hundreds of stars with planets in the "goldilocks zone" discovered starting in the early twenty-first century. These three were discovered thirty to forty years ago, with planets where there was the most evidence for Earth-like climate, closest to Sol. Others were either less likely to have planets like Earth or were much further away. But the truth was, there wasn't much they knew. They'd sent probes to each, and ships on route would get that information—it was possible, even likely, that the planet they were sent to would be uninhabitable. In that event, the ship had enough fuel to take one more trip to another possible star, further away from Sol. If that one was uninhabitable as well, there wasn't much that could be done. They might be able to figure out how to refuel, but it was definitely a big gamble. That was sobering.

The rest of the day included briefings on life on the ship, which for many sections, including Colony Logistics and Agronomy, would be entirely spent in cryosleep. Those in Flight Engineering, Piloting, Communications, and some other sections would rotate being asleep and awake.

At dinner, Henry, Cayenne, Joel and Trina were sitting together at one of the tables in the cafeteria. It was pizza night, Trina's favorite. She hardly ever got pizza at home, it was a special treat, but here, there was pizza every week, on Fridays. And it was really good pizza, too.

Henry said, "What do you all think about that thing about humans becoming extinct? Is that really possible?"

Joel said, "Nah. I think it's possible that we might have screwed up the climate so much that it will be really hard to maintain the same kind of life that we've gotten used to, and I can imagine the population being decimated, or worse. But I can't imagine us making ourselves extinct."

Cayenne said, "I think it's possible. Ever heard of the 'Runaway Greenhouse Effect?'"

Trina asked, "Runaway Greenhouse Effect?"

"Yup. Basically, Venus is hot as hell, I mean literally. Surface temperatures are like 450 degrees c. And it's that way because the atmosphere is 95% CO2. Some scientists are afraid that if the feedback loop that is making the planet get warmer and warmer gets out of control, that we'll end up having a climate like Venus. Nothing could survive that."

Joel said, "Yeah, but we're not as close to the sun as Venus. I don't think it could get that hot."

"It doesn't have to get that hot. Humans certainly couldn't survive a climate where the average temperature was even 70 or 80 degrees c."

Joel said quietly, "You have a point, there."

Trina said, "I hate the possibility that we might have done that to ourselves. I guess I'm glad I get to be part of something that might end up saving us."

Cayenne said, "Me too."

As launch date approached, life got more hectic. They had to squeeze in training and briefings with the work they needed to do to make sure that when they would have what they needed when they arrived.

The ship had been built in orbit, and all sorts of things had been sent to orbit using the Kepler Exploratory spaceplanes. Weight was a big issue and figuring out the best kinds of building materials for an unknown climate had been a challenge. They settled on two strategies, they would build yurts, made out of a new kind of fabric that was plastic and metal mesh, and very light but durable and insulating, with light aluminum frames. The floors would be made of a light plastic tile. They also were shipping up several kinds of catalysts that would allow them to make cement out of available resources on the planet. The yurts would be temporary, and the idea is that they would make permanent dwellings out of available resources on the planet.

One day, Trina was looking over what she hoped was the final report. It looked like the last shipment of catalysts had made it to the ship. She wanted to review it all with Joel, so she went to look for him. She found him talking with Ryenne. He looked at her as she approached.

"Hey, Trina, speak of the devil."

Trina wondered what they were saying about her. "Wish to share?"

Ryenne said, "Joel was just waxing on about how amazing you are."

Trina blushed. "Thanks, Joel."

He said, "I was serious. I had originally been completely against getting anyone from LSI, but you proved me completely wrong." He smiled. "You have something for me?"

"Yup, the final report on the yurt materials and catalysts. We now have 250 kilos of each kind of catalyst. That should be more than enough for worst-case scenarios. And, we have materials for 125 small yurts, 45 medium-sized yurts, and 30 large yurts, for community buildings."

"Do you have any questions about it?"

"No, I'm confident of it. The RFID tags on all of these shipments have been confirmed to be on board the *Precious Hope*. I've been following the shipments since they left the factory. But I would like you to go over it just in case I missed something."

"OK, send it along to me, I'll give it a look."

"Thanks, Joel." It looked like Joel and Ryenne still had business, so Trina left. She still hadn't done her training workout today, and it was getting late.

The next evening at dinner, Trina looked for an empty table, and sat down with her tray of food. She wasn't really in the mood to talk to anyone. Last night, she'd had yet another vivid dream about her family, and woke up thinking she was still at home. Then, her work that day had been frustrating, and her workout much more laborious than usual. It just hadn't been a good day. She ate slowly, trying hard to push away the sad feelings.

"Hey Trina, can I speak with you a moment?" Trina looked up to see Joel standing across the dining table from her. She nodded, and he sat down.

"You don't look so good today. Are you OK?"

She sighed. "I'm fine. Just not having a good day."

"I'm sorry. Do you want to talk about it?"

"No, Joel, not really. But thanks."

"OK. Look, I have to ask you some nosy questions, and I'm apologizing in advance. Some guy from security had some questions about you that I couldn't answer."

"Security?"

"Yeah. They are paranoid and think pretty much everyone is out to get them."

"So, what questions?"

"You worked for CalSpace Tours?"

"Yeah. I was in sales."

"When?"

"From 2099 to 2102, when my parents were killed."

"Did they recruit you for that job?"

"No, I applied. There were a lot of applicants. I tested well and did well at the interview."

"Did you ever meet with anyone from corporate?"

"You mean higher up than my boss?"

Joel nodded.

"No."

"You said you talked to an investor of Solar Exploratory, who flagged your name. Who was it?"

"Let me remember… Nils… Something Nilsson. I don't remember his first name."

"OK, thanks, Trina. I hope that will satisfy them."

Trina nodded.

"You sure you're OK? Maybe you should take a couple of days off."

"And do what, Joel? It's OK, work is good for me."

"Alright. Really, talk to me anytime."

"Thanks." Joel got up and left Trina alone with her thoughts.

Journal, June 4, 2103

Tomorrow is the big day we've all been waiting for. The last six months of training has led up to this: we get on the spaceplane to go to the ship, and get inside a cryosleep pod, and wake up twenty years from now.

The last few weeks have been a lot easier for me. I feel like I've finally hit my stride and gotten used to the situation. The dreams of my family have been replaced with other kinds of dreams. I've made a lot of good friends and have learned a ton of stuff about things I never thought I'd learn. I decided that I would train to become a part of the Science team. Dr. Cassidy Duree, the head of the Science team, said that she would welcome me once they were open to taking new members, and Logistics didn't need me anymore.

I have learned a lot about biology, chemistry, and physics—learned about the kinds of questions we'll be faced with, and the kinds of possible scenarios we might encounter. I am excited about what might be on the other side of cryosleep. What awaits us will be amazing, whatever it is.

I am scared of cryosleep, though. I read the detailed studies, as well as reports on what it was like for people. It is safe, and I'm not worried about anything going wrong. I'm just scared about how it's going to feel. I don't like the idea of feeling like I'm dying.

Takeoff: June 2103

The time was finally here. It was time to go into space. Trina was strapped into her seat on the spaceplane with thirty-five other of her colleagues. This was the last trip to the ship from the compound in Nevada, and once they took off, these would be her last moments on Earth.

The past week had been hectic and chaotic, and she'd hardly gotten any sleep. She could not have imagined how much work it would take to put all of this together, and she knew that she only understood a small piece of it—the work of her section.

When they arrived, most of her job would be building yurts. She didn't mind, really, and they'd practiced building a few of the yurts, so that it would be easier to do once they arrived. Of course, they really had no idea what things would be like once they got down to the planet… if they got down to the planet at all. There was no guarantee it would actually be habitable.

"Prepare for takeoff."

Everyone was strapped in, and Trina had a window seat, and she could see the compound in the distance. The plane started to accelerate down the runway, and Trina just watched out of the window while the compound receded in the distance, and the landscape moved past the window. Soon, the plane angled upward, and Trina could feel herself pushed back hard into the seat. They flew past clouds, and then went above the clouds.

She heard, "Prepare for fusion rocket ignition."

She knew that this meant that they would be tilting at a very high angle and blasting the fusion rocket so they would enter orbit. She braced herself while that happened, and felt the tug of more than four gees, then the sky got dark. After a short time of high gravity, Trina could feel that she was weightless, although she didn't move anywhere, as she was still strapped in. She heard the sounds of several people vomiting. She didn't feel any ill effects herself.

It seemed to take forever, but eventually Trina saw the huge bulk of the *Precious Hope*. In fact, it would have been impossible to tell how big the ship was, but she knew how big it was, from briefings and data on cargo capacity. The engine and fuel took up more than half of the length of the ship, and the cargo holds took up another 40%, leaving about 5% of the ship for command and control, 110 cryosleep pods, and living quarters for about 10 crew who would be awake at any one time.

None of the crew were going to be awake for the full twenty years. Most, like Trina, would be asleep for the entire trip. About forty crew would rotate, each spending about five years awake. The captain and executive officer would each spend 10 years awake.

The spaceplane sidled up to the *Precious Hope*, and Trina lost her view.

"Prepare for arrival."

Someone Trina hadn't met floated in the front of the plane.

"OK, folks, get your packs, strap them on, use the handholds, and follow me."

Trina waited for her seat mates to unstrap and open the cargo container above their heads. Joel passed her pack to her. She strapped it on, then followed the crowd, out of the plane, onto the ship. She was trying to remember the layout of the ship. She thought that the cryosleep area was not really far from the dock.

Everyone on this trip was going straight to cryosleep. This last flight was made up of Colony Logistics, Agronomy and Animal Husbandry. The group of them had a lot of joint meetings, as their work overlapped.

It was strange floating in mid-air. Trina couldn't quite have imagined what it would have been like. She followed people down a passageway that had handholds on each side. Eventually, they ended up in a very narrow room that had rows of lockers.

"OK, undress here, and stow your clothes and packs in the locker assigned to you. It's by ID number."

Trina found her locker, put her pack in the back, then undressed and carefully placed her clothes so that they would be easy to get to when she woke up. She was surprisingly not embarrassed, although she was surrounded by other naked bodies, something that had never happened to her before. She then followed the crowd out of that room, and into a space that had the cryosleep pods, stacked six high.

"Find your pod. Inside is a small canister, holding the tranquilizers and supplements, and a big bottle of water with some important chemicals. Take all of the pills, and drink all of the water, then lie in the tank. Someone will come to assist you."

Trina found her pod. It was the third up from the bottom. All of the other pods in this column already had occupants. She could see them floating in the yellow liquid, with tubes coming from varied places in their bodies.

She knew the basic principle. She would be suspended in a specially formulated liquid, which would also fill her lungs, and allow oxygen into her bloodstream. The liquid would be cooled to very near freezing, slowing her metabolism down to a crawl, and placing her into something akin to a coma. There was a supply of basic nutrients into her bloodstream, as well as a catheter for urine. They had not had anything solid to eat in over a week, which had been quite challenging for just about everyone, including her.

She opened the pod and saw the canister with about 10 pills. She didn't know what all of them were, but it didn't really matter. She took them with the water, then drank the whole thing down. She floated for a moment in front of the pod, and then got in. In a little while, she began to feel the effects of the tranquilizers. She was feeling very calm, and happy. She wasn't worried about anything. She thought that this wasn't going to be all that bad.

"Hi, are you all ready?" A very kindly-looking woman was floating next to her pod.

Trina nodded.

"Alright. First, I need to catheterize you. It will be simple and quick. Please spread your legs as far as they can inside the pod."

Trina did that. The woman pulled a flexible tube from one end of the pod and used her gloved hand to find the right placement for the catheter. Trina hardly minded.

"OK, that's done. Now for the IV. Please hold out your arm."

She took pulled another tube from the other end of the pod and attached a needle to it. She used a tourniquet, just like Trina had had before when she needed a blood test for something. She found the vein, used a strange device that basically shrink-wrapped that part of Trina's arm with the IV.

"Alright. Let me just run the diagnostics, and make sure both of these are right. They need to work for twenty years, you know."

The woman disappeared from view. Trina was drifting, almost getting close to sleep. The woman's voice brought her back to awake.

"OK, we're all set. Put in the earplugs now."

Trina found the earplugs and put them in her ears—she knew that they protected her ears from the liquid, and also they were wired, so that people could communicate with her.

"Now, it's time for the hard part. I'm going to start the liquid flowing. It's a little cold, although not nearly as cold as it will be later. I will be closing this cover, and you'll hear me through your earplugs, OK?"

Trina nodded. Might as well get this over with. The woman closed the pod door, and Trina realized that it wouldn't open again for twenty years. That seemed like a very long time.

The liquid started to flow into the pod, forming odd rivulets in zero gravity. It was pooling toward her feet, and she could feel the liquid now. It was very cold and made her shiver. Then, her legs were increasingly covered, and she got even colder. Once the liquid was at her waist, she was sort of used to it, but occasionally she'd feel how cold it was again.

"When the liquid reaches your mouth, I need you to stretch your head and exhale your breath, as much as you possibly can, then hold your breath and push that button near your hand, OK?"

Trina nodded. She'd remembered this in the briefing on cryosleep, and she felt for the button, so she knew where it was. She lost track as the liquid moved up her torso and chest, but was brought back to attention by the sharp, nasty taste of the liquid in her mouth. She stretched and exhaled, then held her breath, then pushed the button. The pod filled suddenly with liquid, and there was no air left. Her body struggled, knowing that when she inhaled, it would be the liquid. She was suddenly terrified.

Finally, her body gave out. She inhaled and was sure she was about to die. Her chest was burning and she tried to cough, but couldn't. She thrashed about, banging her hands and feet on the walls of the pod. She then felt like she was going to lose consciousness. Something changed, and she was able to exhale, and then she inhaled, and exhaled again. She was breathing, and she clearly wasn't dead. With each exhale came some bubbles, which seemed to be drawn away from her somehow. It was strange breathing liquid. It was a lot more work, but it clearly did the job.

"OK, that was the worst of it, Trina. You'll be fine. I'm injecting the sleeping agent now, and we're cooling down the liquid. You'll be asleep in about a minute or two."

She was thinking about what it would take to make a liquid a human could breathe, and what she'd learned about fluid dynamics in her physics class came to mind, like taking viscosity into account, and oxygen saturation…

In a moment, she found herself in her old apartment again, but it was empty. She couldn't figure out how she'd gotten back home. She sat on the old couch, the fold-out couch that her Nana and grandfather slept on. Suddenly, the door opened, and her parents walked in, with a tree, and lots of presents.

"Trina, its Christmas! We got a big tree this year!"

Awake Again: May 2135

She dreamed many dreams and lived many lives. She was sitting on a cliff, having just climbed it, looking at the Nevada sky, when she heard Cayenne's voice.

"Trina."

She looked toward where the voice had come, but she didn't see her.

"Trina."

The Nevada sky became yellow, and the cliff melted away. She opened her eyes. She was floating in the pod. The liquid was gone. She took a breath, and all she could do was cough. Big drops of yellow liquid were ejected from her mouth with each painful cough.

"It's OK, it takes a while. Just let it happen."

She coughed and tried to breathe for what felt like hours. Finally, she was breathing relatively normally. She saw the pod door open, and Cayenne was floating by her pod.

"Hey girl, time to get you out of this. You're one of the last of our team out."

Cayenne helped her take out the catheter, and the IV, and she floated out of the pod. It was a good thing there wasn't any gravity, she thought. There was no way she'd be able to stand up.

"Let's get you to the shower."

Cayenne pretty much pulled Trina to the shower, which was a vertically-oriented pod with water sprays on three sides. Cayenne put Trina in and closed the door. The water felt luxuriously warm, and Trina could tell it was rinsing all the liquid off of her body. She felt her head—her hair had grown out by at least four inches. Her nails were so long they curled under. The water finally stopped, and hot air jetted around the pod, until Trina was mostly dry.

The door opened, and Cayenne pulled her out, and handed her a jumpsuit.

"Put this on. You'll be wearing it until you're ready to go down to the surface. And let's trim your hair and nails, shall we?"

Cayenne gave her a pair of nail clippers, and Trina clipped her long finger- and toe-nails while Cayenne used electric clippers to bring Trina's afro down to about 1/4 inch in length.

Trina asked, "Have you been down?"

Cayenne shook her head. "Not yet. I just got out two days ago. We'll be going down together in about five days. Joel, Hakim and Henry are down, investigating with the Exploratory team. There are a couple of things you should know at the beginning. First, this isn't Kepler 75f. On route, we got a signal from the first ship—Kepler 75f was not going to be habitable."

"What was wrong?"

"I haven't read the details, and honestly, it doesn't matter. We left, and took off for the second choice planet, where the first ship headed. Kepler 89b. But it's not looking so great, now."

"What do you mean? Not habitable?"

"Oh, no, not that—it's very habitable. Almost perfect, in fact. The atmosphere is breathable, very close to Earth. The climate is mostly tropical, with some more temperate zones near the poles. There's lots of land, and fresh water. It looks ideal, really. The problem is that we found the first colony."

"And?"

"It was destroyed, and we can't find anyone alive. There are some remains, but it can't be the remains are of the entire colony population."

"Can you tell what happened?"

"No. No clue. It happened about ten months after they landed. It looked like one catastrophic event, but we can't figure out what it was. The log on the ship in orbit suggested everything was fine, until the logs just suddenly ended. One day, it seemed everything was normal. The next day, nothing."

"So, what does this mean for us?"

"Not sure yet. I think they need to figure out whether it is something that is possibly avoidable."

"That makes sense. Wait—that means it has been more than 20 years!"

"Yup. Thirty-two years. It's 2135."

Trina didn't quite know what to say. She made her way, with help from Cayenne, to her locker, where she dressed. They went back to the recovery area, where there were exercise machines. Cayenne grabbed a tube of something and handed it to Trina.

She said, "It's a nutritious, but awful-tasting paste you need to eat for a few days before we can eat anything real."

"Gotta taste better than that yellow liquid I've been tasting for thirty-two years."

Cayenne laughed. "Well, yes, it does taste better than that."

Trina took the tube and squeezed the paste into her mouth. It tasted slightly medicinal, and a bit salty. It wasn't too bad. Maybe it got worse over time.

"So, we have only one job—get ourselves ready to work on the planet after all those years of not using our muscles. You'll start on this lovely looking device. It does most of the work."

Cayenne strapped Trina into a seat on top of a robotic-looking thing. Her arms and legs were strapped onto their own articulated robot limbs. Once she was strapped in, it started to move her arms and legs around, in repetitive patterns.

"You'll stay on that for a few hours, then it will be time for some sleep. I gotta go do my own training in the centrifuge. I'll be back to take you out later."

Trina nodded and watched Cayenne move into a large circular machine that started to spin. As it sped up, Cayenne was pulled outward, and was soon standing. She started to walk inside of it. It was odd to watch, but Trina knew it was next for her, probably tomorrow. In the meantime, having her limbs moved about without her own volition was very strange.

Journal Entry, May 15, 2135

I've been out of cryosleep for three grueling days. I spend all of my waking hours either in that contraption that moves my limbs for me, walking in the centrifuge, or doing resistance exercises. I do feel a lot stronger than I did when I first woke up, and since there isn't much gravity except in the centrifuge, which maxes out at .6g, I don't have a real sense of my strength, but I expect it will be a long while before it is back to where it was before.

The living quarters are pretty cramped, but it's good to know that this is temporary. Soon, I'll have a whole planet to roam around on. And, in any event, I couldn't go very far in the shape I'm in.

Cayenne has been around a lot, helping me out. All of the rest of our crew are down on the surface. There are several from other teams still here, and I've gotten to know a couple of people from Science, which has been fun. They seem to like me, and I enjoy talking with them.

At least while I'm doing some exercises I can read, and I got a chance to read the full reports about Kepler 75f, our original destination. It had an active biosphere, but it just had too much carbon dioxide and carbon monoxide for us to live there. There was a very lively argument about whether to stay and try to build domes and the like, but that was ruled out, unless Kepler 89b was much worse. That comment in the report seemed odd, since I know that we wouldn't have had the fuel to go back.

We'd gotten the probe data and the first set of transmissions from the colony during the flight from Kepler 75f to 89b. Kepler 89b is habitable and looked like it would be a good place for a thriving colony. It has an atmosphere that is breathable—it has a bit more of some things than others, but it has enough oxygen, and not too much of compounds that are toxic. It appeared that the planet shares the same carbon and oxygen cycle as Earth: plants that use carbon dioxide, to produce oxygen, and animals that breathe oxygen and excrete carbon dioxide.

The probes found several types of small animal life, which the first explorers confirmed. The probes had found no evidence of intelligent life—no cities, or radio emissions of any sort. The first colony had been quite confident of their success in the logs that I read.

Until... until the first colony just got destroyed, for no reason that anyone could ascertain. It appeared that whatever happened to them happened within the first year of landing, almost five years ago. The only remains of the colony are the vestiges of the landing vehicles, pieces of smashed equipment, and some bones, but not enough bones to account for all of the crew. There was no evidence that any crew were scattered elsewhere on the planet, and there were scouting overflights looking for people, but nothing was found. It was assumed that everyone was dead, and their remains eaten by local scavengers.

Well, it isn't my job to worry about it—my job is to build yurts and there are a lot of yurts to build. Everyone is on edge about happened to the first colony, and it scares me.

Getting Down: May 2135

Trina ate her meal, the last one before she'd be down on the surface, with gravity. She and the rest of the crew were leaving the ship very soon. She was looking forward to it.

"Just about ready?"

Trina looked to see Cayenne floating near her.

"Yup, finishing up my meal. When do we leave?"

"Momentarily. The captain is tying things up here, and then we'll be ready to go. When you're done, you should make your way to the shuttle dock."

"OK, will do."

Cayenne floated away toward the shuttle dock, her pack strapped on her back. Trina squeezed the last of the meal out of the tube, then tossed it into the recycler. She grabbed her pack, and followed in the direction that Cayenne had gone, and arrived at the shuttle dock to see a few others joining them. The shuttle was small and cramped—nothing like the spaceplane that had brought them up from Earth's surface. It had very utilitarian benches with straps, and people were squeezed in. There were no windows. Trina found an open space, put her pack underneath the bench, and strapped in.

"Leaving in five minutes." That was the captain's voice. This was the last shuttle down to the surface—no one would stay aboard ship. And there wasn't any reason to. There wasn't much fuel left—certainly not enough to go anywhere.

Once everyone was aboard, the trip down to the surface was fairly uneventful. For a while, it was bumpy and rough, and Trina knew this meant they were in re-entry. It smoothed out, and they finally touched down on the surface.

Trina knew that the gravity of this planet was about 1/2 of the gravity of Earth, but she couldn't really tell, probably because she'd been in cryosleep for so long, and the centrifuges hadn't worked at higher than .6g. She hefted her pack, which felt heavy enough, and walked out with everyone onto the surface.

She was struck by how different the scene that faced her looked. They were on some sort of grassland or prairie, but the color of everything was off, just a little. The sky had a violet tinge to the blue, and the grasses were a glowing greenish yellow color she'd never seen before. There were strangely shaped rocky hills to the distance in one direction, and a forest of tall trees fairly far away in the other direction. There were a few very tall trees within the area of their camp, and from this distance, Trina assessed them as very unusual, but very climbable.

Joel walked up to them.

"Trina, Cayenne, welcome down. We have a load of work to do. People are clamoring for their personal yurts, my friends. We've got the colony design finalized, after long negotiations with security."

"Security?"

"They've come to the conclusion that the first colony was destroyed by saboteurs."

"Saboteurs? That came on the ship?"

"Yup. Apparently, the investors have enemies. Security is worried about more saboteurs on this ship, as well as the possibility that the saboteurs from the last colony ship are waiting for us."

Trina said, "Oh. Wow."

"Yeah. Which reminds me, security wants to interview you."

"Me?"

"Yeah. For some reason they are concerned about you. I tried to convince them otherwise, but they didn't listen. You need to report to security before you start building yurts. Lemme take your pack, I'll stow it for you."

"Thanks." Trina handed Joel her pack.

"Security is in the medium-sized yellow yurt on that side."

Trina saw the yurt and nodded.

"OK." She walked toward the yurt, bemused. She couldn't figure out why they would be worried about her. And the idea that the previous colony was destroyed by saboteurs seemed sort of far-fetched.

As she approached the yurt, she could see two men in uniforms outside of the door of the yurt. She approached one of them.

"Trina Dewing. I understand you want to see me?"

He nodded and tilted his head a couple of times toward the door. She took that to mean she should walk in, so she did. There was a man sitting at a makeshift desk, looking at several tablets at once. When she entered, he looked up.

"Ah, Trina Dewing. I'm Sergeant Mason, head of security. Thank you for coming so promptly. It would have been unfortunate had we had to find you ourselves." It was said coldly, with malice.

"How can I help you?"

"I understand you worked for CalSpace Tours before you 'sold your labor contract' is that correct?" It was odd, how he inflected the phrase about the labor contract. As if it was a fiction.

"Yes. I was in sales."

"I see. And what exactly did you do in sales?"

Trina described it.

"What do you know about Quirin Nilsson?"

"He was someone I spoke to on the phone, selling a space tour. It turned out he was an investor in Solar Exploratory, and because of our conversation, he flagged my name in their personnel database. He's the reason I'm here."

"And why did you call him?"

"He was on my list of leads, and a very likely one to bite for a tour. He was rich, single, and adventurous."

"I see." She could tell he felt frustrated.

"Alright, tell me about your 'family.'" Again, an odd inflection. She didn't understand what was going on. Somehow, he believed that she was acting?

"I lived in Brooklyn with my parents, Nana and grandfather, great-grandmother, and my little sister, Mita."

"According to your records, your labor contract was sold when your parents were killed in an accident?"

For some reason, it all came flooding back to her—almost as if it had happened yesterday, not thirty-three years before. Some part of her knew that in her own reality, it had been much less than a year, but that didn't stem the tide of the tears flowing. She remembered so vividly her dreams during cryosleep of her parents and family.

"Sorry," she said, embarrassed about crying, "It's still a little fresh for me. Yes, they went dancing one night—they hadn't been dancing for years. The dance floor collapsed, and they died with about twenty others. It was in the news."

"What was the date?"

Trina thought quickly. "December 20, 2102."

The man did something on one of the tablets he had with him. Trina imagined they must have copied a lot of the 'net for him to be able to search the news or death records here. He was silent for a while. He then looked up at her.

"Alright, you check out for now. But know this: there is enough suspicious about your background that you are being watched."

Trina didn't know what to say. Finally, she said, "OK, whatever," and shrugged her shoulders. She left the yurt feeling dismissed. The feeling of his suspicion stayed with her for a while, as she found the yurt that was to be her living quarters for a while. She was sharing it with Cayenne and Bridgit, a woman from Animal Husbandry who had also gotten out of cryosleep during the last shift. She'd gotten to know Bridgit a little bit and enjoyed her company.

Bridgit, like Cayenne, had worked for Planetary Exploratory before coming on this mission. Bridgit was much closer to Trina's age. She'd been stationed on the moon and had been part of an effort to raise chickens in the moon colony. Apparently, it was somewhat of a disaster—chickens did not take to low gravity well at all. It was hoped that 1/2 gravity might be enough for them, but they would start out with ducks, who did much better in lower gravity environments.

She arrived at the yurt, which was currently empty of occupants. She found her bunk, which had her pack on top of it. She spent a little time unpacking: re-folding her clothes, and storing them in the drawers under the bunk, taking out her tablets, and the few personal items she'd accumulated during training, like a gorgeous small stone she found during the climb up the cliff, a photograph of her family she'd surreptitiously printed from an old 'net account she'd had, and a woven yarn bracelet that Cayenne had made her, and put them on the small shelf of the locker next to her bunk.

She felt a wave of fatigue, and she decided to take a short nap. She was awoken by Cayenne shaking her gently. "Time for breakfast."

She was groggy. "Breakfast?"

"Yeah. You slept all night."

She shook her head, as if to rid it of the cobwebs that were clogging it. "Wow, I must have been beat."

"Not a surprise. I'm surprised I managed to stay awake for the poker game. Anyway, we have a long day ahead of us, friend. Yurts to build."

Trina nodded. "Oh, where are the showers?"

Cayenne laughed. "Showers? You're kidding, right? They put up the port-a-potties over on the right side of this group of yurts, you can't miss them. Right outside is a set of sinks running off of some water tanks. You get a trickle for brushing your teeth and washing up. No showers for months, probably."

Trina wrinkled her nose but remembered belatedly the kind of infrastructure showers involved. Infrastructure she'd be helping to build soon enough.

Cayenne added, "Feel lucky you aren't on the port-a-potty crew. Henry got the short straw on that one."

Trina nodded, and thought, yeah, that would not be any fun. She got up, and changed her clothes, and then went to wash up before breakfast. The mess had been set up in the largest yurt so far erected. It was nice to finally eat some solid-ish food that wasn't in a tube. It wasn't especially tasty, though, but when she remembered it was made from dehydrated or vacuum-packed thirty-year-old food, she realized it actually didn't taste too bad. She did look forward to when they could have real eggs, and real vegetables and fruit, but that probably wouldn't be for a long time.

"Hey." Bridgit sat next to her, tray in hand, smiling broadly.

"Hi." Trina smiled in return. She was glad Bridgit was there.

"I hope I didn't wake you last night when I got back to the tent."

"No, I was sleeping the sleep of the dead. I missed dinner."

"I wish I hadn't stayed up so late. I'm already tired this morning."

"What were you up to?"

"Well, I took a walk to the stream on the west side of the colony. Just for curiosity. I almost got lost trying to get back."

"Yikes."

"Yeah, it was stupid. But I was curious. I did find something I'm reporting to Security."

Trina was surprised. She said, "What?"

"Some more human remains."

"Oh!"

"Yeah, there were a bunch of them, sort of randomly strewn. Probably the work of scavengers."

"But I thought all of the animals they knew about were too small to move big pieces of people around."

Bridgit said, "Yeah, I know. But maybe they were wrong."

"Maybe. This whole thing about saboteurs…"

"I know. It makes no sense to me. There would have been more evidence, I think."

"But I can't imagine what else it might have been. But somehow…"

"Well, it's not our worry, right? We are just here to build stuff."

Trina smiled. "Yes, and off to grunt duty we should go, eh?"

They got up, disposed of their trays and utensils in the varied recycling bins set aside for particular items, and went to find Joel. That day, and many days after ran together in a blur. It took her several days to finally stop flopping exhausted into bed after a day of work, until she felt that she had enough energy for the various leisure activities springing up in the colony.

Journal Entry, June 5, 2135

I like this planet and love my work. I spend most days building yurts according to the plans that have been finalized for the colony design. Everyone is anxious to have their own space, their own place to call home, including me, and we're trying to build yurts as fast as we can.

Poor Henry got sewage and plumbing duty, which is less than fun. He's been mostly digging trenches for piping and sewage lines. For now, we've been setting up septic filtering systems. It will be a while before we can actually build a real sewage treatment facility.

Henry says that the water table is relatively close to the surface, and the early wells that were built should serve us for a long time, especially if we are good at conserving water. We don't even really know what season it is right now, and what the seasons will look like. Science suggests that it's likely to be more like rainy/dry seasons, because of the mild tilt to the planet. But we really won't know until we experience a whole year here on Johannes.

I do spend as much time as I can exploring as far as I can. We aren't allowed to go beyond a certain perimeter if we are not part of a specific exploratory team, so I spend most of my time climbing trees. The trees are very tall, and you can see quite far when you are high up. It's amazing, the life here. It's so different than life on Earth, yet it is familiar, as well. The colors and shapes are different, but there are trees, and flying things, and little animals that live underground, like moles.

I have at times gone as close to the forest as I can, sneaking past the perimeter at times when people are busy. There are all sorts of plants that grow closer to the forest, and I love the trees. They almost seem like they are more alive and conscious somehow than trees at home. I know that's weird to say, but when I climb them, I almost feel like they know I'm there. I've also spent time at the stream on the west side of the colony and have found some interesting creatures in the water. I can't wait until we are allowed to go further.

68   MAXWELL PEARL

Suspicions: July 2135

They had finally finished building all of the yurts they would need for the time being and were beginning to scope out plans for the first greenhouses. The Exploratory and Science teams had determined that the soil was arable, and wouldn't need a lot of work or modification, but it was hard to know this for sure without trying. They would use greenhouses first, then try open planting. It would likely be a year before they were able to bring any of the embryos out of storage. Trina had always wanted a dog, and she hoped she'd be able to get one.

Security had been a major pain—they had come to the conclusion that saboteurs had destroyed the first colony, so everything having to do with placement of buildings had to be run through them. It caused major headaches and delays in their schedule. Trina didn't think that this explanation made much sense, given the evidence. And Trina could tell that Security was still suspicious of her, and she didn't really understand why. Joel had told her that they ordered him to send weekly reports on her behavior.

Besides that, she enjoyed the planet that they had now named Johannes, the first name of Johannes Kepler. The climate of this particular area of the planet, which was north of the equator, was very mild, and the temperature wasn't too hot for Trina. Some members of the crew complained of the heat, especially during the early afternoon, but she didn't mind. She couldn't imagine what it was like closer to the equator, though. The gravity was about 1/2 Earth's gravity, which meant everything was easier. Days were slightly longer than Earth days, close enough not to disrupt eating or sleeping patterns, but long enough to feel like one could get more done in a day.

There were lots of native plants and small animals, although no one had so far seen anything larger than a raccoon. The trees were similar to oak trees, in some ways, but they had very strangely shaped leaves that were a very yellowy-green. They grew much, much taller than any oak tree Trina had seen in her life. There were plenty of limbs to climb on, and nice crooks to sit and lie in and relax.

On one of her days off, she'd brought a set of binoculars with her as she climbed one of the trees. She could see a forest far to the east of where they were. She looked out to the forest, and she could see large flying creatures. The binocular measurement suggested that their wing spans could be as large as 5 meters, but that seemed unlikely. She recorded it anyway and would send it to the science team. They certainly had seen flying creatures around the colony - in fact, one of them was considered a major pest, getting into yurts and the like, but it was the size of a bat or sparrow.

She climbed down from the tree and went to the mess yurt. It was time for dinner. They would be eating rations from the ship for at least another few months, or longer. They had enough supplies to eat well for 18 months, and then minimal rations for another six. The plan was that if they weren't able to grow edible crops in 10 months, they'd pack up, and head somewhere else. Based on the data so far, this outcome seemed very unlikely. Science had already found six native plants that were edible, and several members of the colony had already eaten some, to no ill effect so far.

As she approached the mess yurt, she heard behind her, "Trina!" She turned to see Henry trotting up to her.

"Hey Henry! How are the greenhouse plans going?"

"Great, great. I'm so glad to finally get out of plumbing and sewage! We're just about ready to break ground on the first one. In fact, Joel wanted you in on that."

"OK, that's fine. I've been repairing some yurts. It will be nice to do something different."

"Already repairing yurts?"

"Yeah. Mostly due to those small flying creatures getting stuck in them. Not huge problems, though."

"That's good. Hey, we're playing poker again tonight. You in?"

Trina laughed. "Sure!" She remembered the first poker game, back at the training compound. She was the only member of their team who was indentured, and she had absolutely no money. Henry lent her $10, and she was still playing on the winnings. She'd paid him back months ago, and had about $300 in cash, that she used only for poker. What else was she going to use it for? She was good at poker, probably because she was very good at telling when people were bluffing - but she used that talent judiciously enough that people didn't actually know it.

She and Henry walked into the mess yurt, grabbed their food, and sat down, later to be joined by Cayenne and Bridgit.

Cayenne said, "How's the yurt repairs?"

Trina answered, "Going fine. Those flying things do some serious damage to the yurts once they're inside."

"I didn't think they have beaks."

"They don't, but they have two pairs of claws."

"Two?"

"Yeah, they have six appendages, two wings and four legs, each with what looks like four talons."

"Wow. Six limbs. Interesting."

Henry said, "Every animal Science has identified so far has six appendages. Insects on Earth have six limbs, and some even have wings on top of that. Anyway, no reason why evolution couldn't have a result like that."

Cayenne said, "True."

Trina said, "I saw some really big flying creatures out near the forest while I was climbing a tree today. Cousins of our little pests, I bet."

Henry said, "Could be. I've been monitoring Science's reports on flora and fauna. Really interesting stuff. Some things are really similar to Earth, and others, quite different. For instance, the compound in the plants that helps to convert CO_2 is in a totally different kind of setup than chlorophyll. It clearly evolved completely differently from the start."

Trina said, "I'll have to read those. I've been so tired from building I haven't felt that I had much in the way of spare energy, but now that things are a little easier, I should check that stuff out."

Bridgit said, "After months, I finally heard back from Security about those remains I found my first night here."

"Oh?"

"Yeah. They concluded that they were killed with knives, and then later eaten by scavengers. The weird thing is that Science thinks the scavengers had teeth way too large for any creatures we've seen so far."

Trina said, "Why does this not quite add up?"

"Because it doesn't! Science thinks that Security is holding something back, and Security thinks that Science is holding something back. I think there is something they are both missing, but I can't figure out what it is."

Trina said, "I wonder if those big flying creatures I saw today might be scavengers."

Bridgit said, "That could be, but you'd think they would have been flying over this way, kind of like vultures do. How else would they know if there was something to scavenge?"

"Good point."

Cayenne said, "Folks, we're not going to solve this puzzle tonight. Shall we go play poker?"

They all nodded, and got up and disposed of their trays, and went to one of the community yurts that had the table and chairs for a poker game. It was an enjoyable game, and Trina, as usual, managed to win a nice amount. As she was walking back to her yurt after the game, Bridgit touched her on the shoulder.

"How is it that you almost always win? Most of us win some, and lose a lot, but I have yet to see you lose much."

Trina smiled. "My secret."

"C'mon, Trina!"

"If I tell you, you have to promise not to tell anyone."

"OK… you're not…"

"No! I don't count the cards! I mean I could, but I don't."

"Alright! So, what is it?"

"I'm really good at telling when someone else is bluffing. I'm not sure exactly what it is—why I can tell, but I can, and I'm always right. You are especially obvious, but I can tell even when Cayenne is bluffing."

"But you don't always…"

"Then I would give it away, wouldn't I?"

"Well, that's a good talent."

"It clearly serves me well. Not that there is much I can do with the $350 I now have."

"Well, there are several black markets in the colony…"

"Nothing I'm interested in."

"Somehow, that does not surprise me." Bridgit smiled, and they entered their yurt.

The next day, Trina was with Cayenne and Henry. She was holding up a thick aluminum tube, which was part of the frame of the first greenhouse. Trina noticed one of the security guys staring at them as they began to put the greenhouse together. She wondered what that was about.

Soon enough, though, that guy came closer.

"Trina Dewing?"

She looked at him, her hands still holding up the tube while Cayenne and Henry were locking in other tubes that were connected.

"I'm here. I'm a little busy at the moment."

"Sergeant Mason wants to see you, immediately."

"Immediately? You've been standing over there for almost twenty minutes. It can't be all that urgent. Can you let us finish this, please?"

"It's your head."

Trina sighed, and she helped to finish up the first frame for the greenhouse, then she followed the officer back to the Security yurt.

The officer went into the yurt, motioning her to stay outside. In a moment, he came out, and motioned her in.

"Don't you know the meaning of 'immediately,' Ms. Dewing?"

"Well, your guy stood by watching us, and chose the most inopportune moment to let me know you wanted to see me. I was holding up part of a greenhouse frame. I finished that part and came right away."

"That's not what he said. He said it was a challenge to find you."

"He did, did he? Well, that might be because he didn't bother to check the work schedule. I went directly from my bed, to breakfast, to the greenhouse site."

Sergeant Mason looked down at something on his desk.

"I understand that you've been spending a lot of time in one of the trees, with a binoculars. You also have been caught twice going beyond the perimeter. Why is that?"

"I'm curious. I'm watching the forest, and the winged creatures that seem to fly above it. And I've found some new plants and animals on my explorations. I reported it all to Science—you can ask them."

"You are not a member of the Science team, and not assigned to exploration.

"Cassie has said she'd welcome me when…"

"When what? I think it's a great cover for more sinister activities."

Trina sighed and shrugged her shoulders. "If that's what you think."

"I called you here because I got the final download from the colony ship, with more information about that 'accident' your parents were in. It appears that the collapse of the dance floor that killed them is suspicious."

"What do you mean?"

"The report suggested that it was not an accident after all."

Trina was shocked at that, but when she quickly recovered, she could hardly understand why that was relevant. She guessed that perhaps, in a mind that had already decided that she was a saboteur, anything suspicious was evidence.

"And how does that relate…"

"I'm asking the questions here!" Sargent Mason barked. Trina flinched.

"You don't drink." That wasn't a question.

"No. I'm not 21 yet."

"And that stops any of the others your age?"

"I don't really want to drink."

"But you have money, even though you've never been paid."

"I'm a good poker player. A friend of mine lent me $10 once, and I keep winning. I already paid him back."

"Why don't you want to drink?"

"I have seen what it does to people." One of Trina's uncles was an alcoholic, and she had seen what damage it had caused.

"You are still our prime suspect."

"Suspect? For what? I don't understand."

"The last colony was destroyed by saboteurs, and I believe this one is slated to. And you are the one who was supposed to carry it out."

Trina didn't know what to say. She thought that saying 'are you crazy?' would not be an especially good idea at the moment.

"You are dismissed. But you are being watched, every minute."

She nodded. If they wanted to waste their time, so be it. But it didn't matter. She was here, and she was going to do the best she could to make her legitimate place in this colony. She went back to helping build the first greenhouse.

Later that day, she was again up in one of the trees, looking at the forest with binoculars. She wasn't quite sure why it intrigued her so, but it captivated her to watch the flying creatures in the distance. There were never many of them flying together at one time—none of the flying creatures they had found so far seemed to fly in flocks—they all flew in twos and threes—never alone, but never in larger groups either.

The most active time for these flying creatures seemed to be in the middle of the day, when the sun was high in the sky. Late in the day, like now, there were many fewer of them flying.

Once, she saw two of them fly to the edge of the forest and sit at the top of a tree looking toward their colony. She could imagine that perhaps they could see some activity from that far a distance, and she wondered what they made of it.

Journal Entry, August 10, 2135

We've been occupied lately by helping Agronomy set up the greenhouses. We built four of them, and for three, we've built the raised beds, and we began hauling soil from outside into the greenhouses for testing. It's a lot of work, but it feels satisfying.

The fourth greenhouse is set aside for hydroponic crops. They don't know how the soil will work for our food plants, and whether or not it will sustain them, and what sort of additives will be necessary. Hydroponics are almost guaranteed to work, but it is much more energy intensive, and we don't have a lot of energy to spare at the moment.

We haven't been able to finish the big solar arrays—that will take another few months to complete. There are already enough small solar panels installed on top of most yurts to take care of everyday needs, but for agriculture and manufacturing, we'll need the big arrays. It's a little bit of a race for time, and it's been important to prioritize food over energy. But some food production takes energy. Our next job, after finishing the greenhouses will be to start the big solar arrays. Engineering has found the most likely spots in the hills west of the colony.

I ran into Sergeant Mason again, at mess. He always looks at me funny, as do all of his team. I don't know what to do about it. I'm not going to stop my explorations, just because for some silly reason he suspects me of something. It doesn't make much sense to me. I'm trying to ignore it.

Cayenne, Joel, Bridgit and Henry have all been really nice about it. I know they believe me, know I'm no saboteur, and they have my back. That helps a lot. And today, my twentieth/fiftieth birthday, they threw me a nice surprise party after dinner, and it even had cake! That was the first cake I'd had in years. It was very sweet of them.

Destruction: August 2135

Trina was awakened by shouts and loud sounds. She came awake quickly and could see Cayenne and Bridgit running out the door. She put on her shoes and followed them into complete chaos. People were running and there was a lot of dust in the air.

She remembered her emergency training. Teams gathered at specific points in the colony in an emergency. She was on Gamma team and was supposed to head to the medical yurt. She started to run in that direction.

Trina could see other people were running toward the medical yurt, which was on the east end of the colony, fairly far away from Trina's yurt. She slowed down, scared about what was going on. She heard shouts, and some screams, as well as loud pounding noises, loud grunts she could not identify, and noises of equipment being shattered and broken. She found it hard to imagine what could be the cause of all of this chaos. Was it the saboteurs?

As she walked, there was a break in the dust, and she saw an enormous creature, wielding a large dull-colored metal spear. She saw it try to stab someone, who managed to move out of the way. She was having a hard time taking in what she was seeing. It had thick-looking, dark green skin and was bigger than anything Trina had ever seen. She guessed it was more than twice the size of that elephant she saw as a kid in the Bronx Zoo, before they closed it.

It was bipedal, with two thick legs, and it had two pairs of arms. Its head was big, and it didn't have a neck, really. It had very heavy eye ridges. She realized that between the eyes and the lack of a neck, it probably could not see above itself at all.

She then could see many, many more of them, likely more than forty behind the first one. They were bashing down buildings, and spearing people. She watched in horror as one stopped after spearing someone and ripped off a leg to put it in its mouth. The only thing she thought made sense was to climb one of the trees and stay out of these creatures' way. She couldn't imagine anything else to do.

She ran to Cayenne, Bridgit and Henry, who had momentarily paused and looked like they were strategizing.

"Hey, come with me. I think we should climb a tree. I don't think they can follow. We could wait them out."

Cayenne shook her head. "I'm on team Alpha, and I'm going to the security yurt—there are weapons there."

Cayenne ran away, and Henry said, "You go, get out of here. I think I can figure out how to get rid of them." Bridgit shook her head and followed Henry. Trina decided to follow them anyway, but she was afraid, she moved more slowly, and she lost them in the dust ahead. She stopped, just in time to see one of the creatures emerge from the dust and come right at her. She ran to the nearest tree and felt a sharp stab in her leg. She ignored it, and started to climb as quickly as she could, and went as high as possible. She settled onto a branch that she thought was too high for any of the creatures to reach. The one that had tried to catch her was gone.

Her leg started to throb, but she was afraid to look at it to see how much it was injured. She did her best to ignore it. She tried to look around, but she couldn't see much, because of the dust and debris being generated by the huge creatures, but she could hear every crash, and worse, she could hear every scream.

Trina had been in the tree for a long time. She watched as the big creatures finished destroying everything they found and killed everyone in the colony. They were so big that they were able to destroy even the shuttle and lander. Trina could see nothing of substance left standing. There certainly weren't any people left alive.

Except her, of course. She felt an odd sense of shame and relief. She'd been scared out of her mind seeing the creatures bigger than anything she could imagine rip through the colony, surprising everyone. She realized that she had barely come away with her life, though, even though she had been scared into climbing a tree.

The result was that she was, at least, alive. She didn't know how long she would have to wait in the tree. The creatures clearly hadn't seen her. The sun was going down, and the creatures, having seemingly eaten their fill, and done the damage they wanted, were filing out of the destroyed colony, many were carrying things Trina couldn't identify. Trina decided that she'd best spend the night in the tree, so she made herself as comfortable as she could.

Her injured leg hurt, a lot, and she tried her best to ignore it. Strangely to her, the branch she was sitting in started to bend slightly, as if it was conforming to her weight, and making it more comfortable. She didn't really pay it much attention, and she finally fell asleep. She dreamed of home again, of her family. Trina was brought awake by the feeling of someone looking at her. She opened her eyes and looked into an alien face.

It scared her, and she drew back, but it made these gentle cooing sounds, which seemed to calm her down. She looked again.

The face was rather large—it had large eyes that were a beautiful blue color, with no whites, and a deep, dark iris. It had a mouth, with lips, like humans, except… different, darker, and stiffer, perhaps. Its body, which was very large, was feathered, and it was all brown, and it had a small crest on top of its head. The body was at least three meters tall and almost two wide, which she could now tell had folded wings. It seemed to have two legs with talons, which were curled around a branch of the tree, and two arms with four-taloned hands, although those talons seemed thinner and more delicate and flexible—they looked a lot like fingers. It must be one of those flying creatures she saw above the forest in her binoculars. It must have flown to this tree.

She heard another cooing sound above her, to see a second one of them sitting on some branches further away from her. They hadn't killed her yet, so she had to assume that they were probably more curious than anything. She knew that the big creatures that destroyed the colony didn't have any technological accoutrements except for some sharp metal spears, but they were intelligent, and worked together as a unit. She had no idea whether or not these bird-things were intelligent, but maybe she could find out.

She pointed to herself. "Trina."

The one closest to her said, "Treena" in an oddly inflected voice, but completely intelligible. Trina noticed that they stretched out the long vowels, much, much longer than was done in English.

She pointed to it. It pointed a talon to itself and said, "Zolweeva."

She said, "Zolweeva." It cooed.

She pointed to the one above, who said, "Keeliza." She repeated that, and they both cooed.

The first one, Zolweeva, pointed down, and said, "Hukoovo."

Trina didn't know what this word referred to. Was it the big creatures?

Trina tried her best to make herself like one of them, and said, "Hukoovo." It cooed again. She was right. She realized it would take a long time to learn how to speak with them this way, but then, that was all she had now, was time.

She did need to get down from this tree at some point soon. She hadn't had anything to eat or drink since the night before. She motioned climbing down, and Zolweeva made a different sound, one not so pleasant. This suggested to her that it wasn't safe yet.

Zolweeva pointed to its back, and moved up the branch, and turned around. Trina could see that it had some sort of pouch on its back. It kept pointing, and turning around, and Trina was getting that it wanted her to ride it. She was frightened, but she realized that she didn't really have much in the way of options at the moment. This seemed like the best of the few available to her. They had done nothing threatening, and if this was a ruse to get her to somewhere where they could kill and eat her, it didn't really matter—she was dead anyway if she didn't get out of this tree safely. She stood slowly, grimacing with the pain in her leg, and climbed toward it. It turned around and cooed. She climbed on, and settled herself stomach-down, into the pouch. Zolweeva took off, Keeliza following quickly behind.

She poked her head up above the edge of the pouch and saw the landscape as they were flying. They were heading to the forest, for sure. After a while, several other bird-things were flying around them, and by the time they dropped into the forest, landing on a platform just below the canopy, she was surrounded by five others like Zolweeva and Keeliza. On a couple of them, she could see little heads poking out from behind them—clearly, the pouches were generally used to carry young. They were making a quite a racket.

She assumed the racket was about her. They weren't threatening in any way, in fact, it almost seemed as if they were challenging Zolweeva and Keeliza for the privilege to interact with her. She sat and watched them for a while, and heard the word "Hukoovo" several times, which she imagined pertained to what happened to the colony.

Finally, things settled down, and most of the rest flew off a ways. Keeliza looked at her leg, where the pants were torn, and there was dried blood in a wide streak on her calf. Trina was glad it had stopped bleeding. Another of the creatures handed her a cloth that was wet with water. Trina used it to clean off the wound, grimacing as she did it. It was going to close itself, which was a good thing. She hoped there was nothing that could infect it.

As she finished cleaning the wound, her stomach grumbled. She was very hungry and thirsty. She motioned with her hands, as if to put food in her mouth and drink. Either they would have to feed her, or she'd have to go back to the colony to find some food among the ruins.

Keeliza flew off immediately, and Trina wondered whether she'd done something insulting. But in a few minutes, Keeliza was back, and had a sort of clay bottle, and something wrapped in leaves. Clearly, she was understood.

Keeliza pointed to the jar, and said, "Yooui see zeelay roo".
Trina took the jar, and tilted it, tasting it. It was just water.
She said, "Water."
Keeliza repeated "Water."

Trina drank deeply of it, finishing what was in the jar. She realized as she drank how thirsty she'd been. Keeliza took the jar, flew off, and came back with it full again.

Trina said, "Thank you," and bowed.

Keeliza said, "Thank you?" It was a question.

Trina smiled, pointed to herself and said "I say, 'thank you'," and then she pointed to Keeliza and said, "you say, 'you are welcome.'"

Keeliza cooed. "You are welcome."

Trina realized that they were very smart and learned fast.

Keeliza gave her the leaf-wrapped package, and Trina opened it to see some sort of flesh that looked like fish, and some other small leaves, perhaps herbs in it. She tasted it. It was strange tasting, but not at all bad, and her stomach took over, and she ended up wolfing it down. She hoped there was nothing she'd regret later.

She bowed again. "Thank you."

Keeliza said, "You are welcome," and cooed.

She drank a bit more water, then she felt sated, and almost ready to deal with her new situation. She would eventually have to go back to the colony and retrieve what she could. She hoped that at least she could find a communications unit, so she'd be able to receive the narrow-beam transmissions from Earth sent to Kepler 75 by Kepler Exploratory. She knew that the first colony had put in a repeater, to send the signal to Kepler 89. She also hoped to be able to eventually communicate with whatever ship was on its way here.

She'd need some nutritional supplements, to make sure she didn't end up with any deficiencies. She didn't know whether or not the local food would provide her with everything she needed. The last report from Science suggested that there were several amino acids that were missing from life on Johannes, and she'd have to figure out how to make sure she got enough of them.

But for now, she needed to understand more about these creatures, and what they had in mind for her. She wanted to be able to learn their language and communicate with them. They seemed peaceful and curious, they'd fed her, and seemed to wish to take care of her. She didn't totally trust them—but she did figure that they knew that the "Hukoovo" were dangerous to her, and wanted to protect her from them, and that gave them many points in her internal assessment.

Zolweeva cooed, and walked toward the end of the platform, motioning her to follow. She got up and limped toward Zolweeva, and Keeliza was next to her. When she arrived at the end of the platform, she could see below her a series of platforms, both open and enclosed, built under the canopy, and dozens of other creatures just like Zolweeva moving about. Zolweeva pointed again to its back, and Trina got on again, and they flew a little bit and landed on a platform that jutted out from an enclosed space. They walked inside, and Trina followed.

This must be their house, Trina thought. It was both very familiar, and very strange at the same time. It was quite large, with tall ceilings, of course, since they were large creatures. It was made entirely of wood, although it almost seemed as if the house and even some things in in it were grown out of the wood, rather than constructed. She was standing in what she would think might be a main room. It had some perches, one of which Keeliza flew to and stood on. It also had a table, which had on it a variety of things that were clearly made objects. There were varied clay vessels around, and what looked a lot like books. She picked one up, and Zolweeva cooed, and said "Jeeelota hay nooo seela weevo." Trina opened it and looked at the pages. They were thicker than most paper she'd seen, but there was a kind of written language on the pages, and some drawings. She was stunned to see what was clearly a drawing of right triangle, and what she could swear was the description of the Pythagorean Theorem, even though she couldn't identify the symbols.

She picked up the book and said, "Book." She then pointed to a page and said "Page." Zolweeva cooed, and Keeliza repeated what Trina had said. Trina was curious about the rest of the house. She got up and motioned that she'd like to keep looking. Both Keeliza and Zolweeva cooed, and Zolweeva led her to another room.

This looked likely to be the kitchen. It had something that looked like a clay oven, with some coals that were still going, and a chimney. There were more of the leaves that had wrapped the meat she'd been given, with some green looking vegetables, and a few other things. There were some sharp knives, and more clay vessels, some covered with cloth, others open, or covered with a clay lid.

When she was about 12, she'd gotten really curious about the history of human civilization, and had read just about everything she could find, and understand about it. She figured, based on what she was seeing, that these creatures were about at the equivalent stage of development as humans were in the Bronze Age. They clearly had fire, and metal, and understood a fair amount of mathematics. But she also knew that she could be totally wrong—they could be following a completely different trajectory than humans did.

Zolweeva kept walking, and Trina followed into a room that looked a lot like a chaotic office. She was suddenly reminded of her time during training, and she felt sadness, knowing that Joel, Cayenne, Henry and the rest of her colleagues were dead. Zolweeva came close to her and was looking in her eyes. It cooed, and reached its hand to her face, and touched her tears.

"Gileera seeko wisee fosee. Gileera weeko?"

"I am sad, Zolweeva. These are tears…" she pointed to her face with the tear.

"Tears. I am sad?"

"No, Zolweeva. I am sad." She pointed to herself. "You are not sad." She pointed to Zolweeva.

Zolweeva said, "You are sad. Why tears?"

"My people…" she pointed out the window to other creatures, "are dead by the Hukoovu."

Zolweeva cooed and put one of its hands lightly on her shoulder. She realized it understood how she felt. She looked around the office and could see many books and papers. And she also saw instruments of various kinds that she did not recognize. She hoped she'd get to learn all about what they knew.

She realized abruptly that they weren't scared of her or hadn't treated her like a specimen. She couldn't even imagine how a single alien would be treated on Earth, but it certainly wasn't like this—like a guest. She wished she could ask them why, but she would be able to, soon enough.

Zolweeva walked back into the main room, and Trina noticed two things. No bathroom, and no bedrooms. It made sense to her. They probably slept on the perches in the main room and flew out somewhere to relieve themselves. Trina would have to do something about that for herself.

She made a set of somewhat embarrassing sign language motions for having to climb down to relieve herself, then Keeliza flew out of the house, and Trina was confused. Keeliza came back with a clay vessel, which looked big enough for Trina to sit on. Trina looked inside and saw a kind of green moss inside.

After another set of embarrassing sign language motions and trying to explain words like "private," Keeliza put the clay vessel in the corner of the room and strung a cloth so that Trina would have some privacy.

Keeliza also got together cloths with moss inside for Trina to sleep on. It would do, for now, although it was lumpy and not especially comfortable. But Trina was exhausted, and she fell asleep immediately.

She woke up and saw threads of sunlight streaming into the windows from above the canopy. The house was empty. Trina got up, relieved herself, then walked into the kitchen, where there was a clay plate, with some of the same meat she'd eaten yesterday, and what looked like some cooked seeds. It clearly was put out for her.

She knew that she'd have to go back to the colony to get what she could of supplements and food, as well as testing equipment to figure out what she was lacking. But for now, this food seemed to agree with her, so she ate it.

When she was finishing up, Keeliza walked into the kitchen.

Trina said, "Thank you for the food." She motioned with her hand, bringing it to her mouth.

Keeliza said, "You are welcome. Jeezo liteel groolzo se leezee, looge hee oogsoo."

Trina had no idea what Keeliza was saying.

She said, "I like it," and patted her belly.

"Like it. Jeer jeezo goofi go eel zee oo to ti." Keeliza cooed.

Trina watched while Keeliza went about doing things in the kitchen. Keeliza took Trina's plate, as well as some other clay vessels and plates of varied sizes and used sand from another vessel to scrub them. Then Keeliza turned on a spigot and rinsed them. Trina was curious about the plumbing. Clearly water was being pumped somehow, from somewhere to here. The plumbing looked to be made of a kind of live plant, rather than metal, although the spigot and spout were clearly metallic.

Trina was suddenly frustrated. She couldn't ask Keeliza about the plumbing, because she didn't have the words, or know the words to ask, and she'd never understand what Keeliza answered, anyway. She sighed and tried to make herself be patient.

Keeliza seemed to sense her distress, and cooed, and said something quietly that Trina did not understand. Keeliza then left the kitchen, and she could hear Keeliza and Zolweeva discussing something. Keeliza returned to the kitchen with Zolweeva.

Zolweeva had a book in its hands, and something that looked like a pencil. Zolweeva handed them to Trina. She opened the book, and the pages were blank. Zolweeva pointed to the table, then motioned to her to write something. She then understood. They wanted to learn her language. She bet that they somehow knew that the best thing would be for them to learn English.

She pointed to the table, and said, "Table." She drew a table, then wrote an equals sign, then the word.

Zolweeva said, "Geel ree eer foo wi ei teee to." Trina wondered whether what Zolweeva said was equivalent to "table" or was something else.

Zolweeva pointed to the clay stove, and she said, "Stove," then roughly drew the stove, and then wrote the word. They kept going around the house, then outside, and Trina kept drawing and writing. Sometimes, Zolweeva would take the book back, and write notes, which Trina assumed were pronunciation tips.

Some things were confusing. They clearly had many, many more words than she thought English had, and many more parts of speech, and then there was also confusion about what was generic, and what was specific. They spent a few days cataloging words, and also Trina did her best to explain sentence structure, and verbs, nouns, adjectives, etc. And almost hourly, Zolweeva got better and better. After about a week, they got to a point where Trina felt that they could actually communicate. It was time for her to explain what she had to do next.

"Zolweeva, I need to go back to the colony."

"You need to go back? You need many things." Zolweeva cooed.

"Yes. I need supplements, and equipment." They'd finally straightened out how to talk about equipment—it had been somewhat of a struggle.

Zolweeva said, "Is it safe now it is. Gone Hukoovu away, far away. We fly take you. Keeliza and Zolweeva take you."

Trina nodded. The food and supplements and the varied equipment she hoped to get were likely more than she could carry in a backpack. Keeliza and Zolweeva talked, and Trina could still not understand what they said.

Trina climbed on Zolweeva's back, and they flew back toward the colony. As they circled it, Trina could see the complete devastation. There were no yurts left standing, and there were things strewn all over.

They landed, and Trina first went to where her old yurt was. Pieces of it were strewn about, but she found her bunk. Her backpack and other effects were still in the drawers and locker. She took them all out, and packed up her backpack with her belongings, and anything else around she thought would be useful.

A wave of sadness and loneliness washed over her, and she had to stop packing for a moment. She mourned the loss of her friends and colleagues—it was as if her parents had died, all over again. She collapsed in a heap on the ground, and she felt hands on her shoulder. She looked up to see Zolweeva looking at her, and cooing. Zolweeva's reaction made her feel better, and she wiped off her face, and kept packing.

She next went to where the medical yurt was. Everything was also strewn about, but several cabinets, although overturned, looked basically intact. She realized that she'd need as much in the way of medicine as she could gather. She found some more backpacks and filled a second one with all of the medical supplies that made sense to her.

She then went to where the dining yurt was, but there was almost nothing left of it. She did find many bottles of multivitamins, as well as bottles of amino acid and nutrient supplements, which she packed. It looked like the Hukoovu had taken all of the food—there wasn't any food left at all.

She then went looking for any equipment she could find. Around one of the Science yurts, she found some binoculars, chemical analyzers, a microscope, a spectrophotometer, and about 10 tablets that still looked like they worked. She then found some small solar panels, and batteries that would be charged by them. This would allow her to use any of the equipment she found.

She looked for what felt like hours for any communications devices. She had just about lost hope, when she flipped over a large metal panel on the ground, and found several communications devices, and a bunch of what looked like spare parts underneath. They were badly battered, and most of them seemed to be damaged in one way or another. She hoped she could figure out how to make them work.

She gathered them all up and packed them in another backpack. She now had five backpacks full of stuff. She hefted two, and Keeliza put three on her back, and they flew back to the trees.

When they got back, they flew to a different house than before. It was smaller, and the main room had lot of big pillows on the floor, with heavy cloths that seemed like blankets. There was a corner with some cloth hanging across it, which Trina assumed was the toilet.

Keeliza said, "You now have your own… house."

Trina didn't quite know what to say. She so appreciated the gesture.

"Thank you Keeliza. I appreciate this so much." Trina touched her heart. She had noticed how when Keeliza or Zolweeva expressed appreciation, they touched their chests.

Keeliza cooed, and said, "I get anything you need, Treena."

"Thank you, Keeliza."

Zolweeva and Keeliza left, and Trina wandered around the small house. It, like their house, had a kitchen, and they had left food for her. It also had another small room in the back. Trina decided to re-arrange things, to better suit her. She took the desk that was in the small room out to the main room, and then moved most of the pillows into the small room in the back. She moved her improvised toilet to a corner of the kitchen.

She would make the main room her study and living room, and the small back room her bedroom. She unpacked her backpack with her personal belongings in the bedroom, hanging some things on hooks that were on the walls, and folding others in a corner on the floor. She'd eventually want to make herself some furniture, but that would take a while.

She walked back to the main room and unpacked the backpacks that held the solar panels and batteries. She went outside and looked at the roof. She'd need tools, too. She made a mental note of the things she needed first.

The next day, she was sitting in her main room, looking around. She hadn't yet had been able to set up the solar panels, so the tablets were not useful at the moment. But she wanted to get them going as soon as she could, so that she could go back to recording her journal.

It had been only six days since the attack. The shock was wearing off, but she felt at a loss. What was she supposed to do? What did she want to do? She liked the flying creatures, and they seemed to like her. She wanted to learn more about what they knew, and what their history was.

And she wanted to explore Johannes. She wanted to understand everything she could about the planet, in the hope that the third colony would make it here. She would do her best to make sure it didn't suffer the fate of the first two.

Journal Entry, November 2, 2135

I have a few solar panels set up on the roof of my house, and I've charged some devices, and now I have tablets I can use, including my own. It feels good to be able to write again.

It has been a difficult twelve days since the attack. Whenever I close my eyes, I see over and over the scene with one of the Hukoovu, as these flying creatures call them, eating one of my colleagues. I can't shake the image, no matter what I do.

Zolweeva and Keeliza have graciously given me a house of my own. I can't quite believe it. It's so beautiful, just like their house. It seems to be sort of grown or cultured. It's part of the tree—you can't separate where the tree ends, and the house begins. It's like living inside of a tree trunk, except it's light, since there are a lot of windows, and comfortable.

The plumbing seems also to be some sort of living vine that they have been able to shape into pipes, and it pumps fresh water into the houses, and delivers wastewater down to the ground.

I have been treated with great respect, although I suspect that these creatures are a lot smarter than I am. Even though they live simply, without technology, they have a language that I have not even begun to be able to decipher. Even the simplest things, like a table, or bowl, are made up of many words. And one bowl can be one set of words, and another bowl is another set of words, and there may be no words in common between the two. It's baffling to me.

Luckily, they seem to be picking up English at a rate that is astounding, and we can basically communicate. I appreciate that, but it feels as though I'll never really understand them until I can understand how they speak. And honestly, I fear that may never happen.

Foreigner: January 2136

Trina had started counting the days at the very beginning. Johannes had days that were 27.6 hours long. She knew that about 200 days had elapsed between the time that the colony landed and the attack by the Hukoovu. Eighty days had elapsed since the attack. She finally felt more settled in. She had a routine; she'd built some furniture to make herself comfortable. Everyone had been welcoming to her, and she was constantly showered with food and other gifts.

But she had her days sometimes. Days that felt lost in a mist of sadness. For a long while, Zolweeva and Keeliza would always be around, sort of hovering. She didn't really understand why, and she told them that they didn't need to stay—they could go off and do whatever it was they normally did. She'd be alright on her own.

Now, the Eeriv left her alone many days, and she missed them. But really, she felt the loss of her friends, and, ultimately, her parents. She'd never really had a chance to mourn their loss. She guessed now was the time.

She often felt as if she were faking her confidence—the confidence that she could survive here, and finally even help the new colony make their way without being attacked by the Hukoovu, when (or if) they arrived. But when she sunk into that place of sadness and uncertainty, she had to move herself out of that place by force of will. She had been working hard on the communications equipment and was hopeful that she'd get at least one piece working, the narrow-band receiver. That was better than nothing. She'd gotten many tools from Zolweeva and Keeliza, but some of them were too big for her to use— their hands were more than twice the size of hers. They had even gotten some tools made that would fit her hands better, which she much appreciated.

She had never really been an ace at electronics. She'd learned some on her own and had definitely been the fix-it person of her family, but it wasn't her strongest suit. She knew that if she could find replacement parts from among the stuff she'd gathered, she'd likely be able to fix the receiver. The piece of equipment she assumed was the ship-to-ground transceiver had a badly smashed motherboard, so she'd written it off, and taken it apart, to get whatever usable parts remained of it.

She had the parts strewn about a large table Zolweeva had given her. She had sorted the parts and identified as many as she could from the information and specifications she'd found on the tablets. She was looking for one particular part that had burned out in the receiver when she heard a quiet coo in front of her. She looked up to see Keeliza looking into the house from the platform. Zolweeva was close behind.

"Come in! How are you?" She hadn't seen them in a few days and had wondered where they had been.

Keeliza said, "I am feeling well, Treena. How are you?"

"I'm struggling to put this equipment together. It was never anything I was very good at, but I'm trying to learn. Luckily, one of the tablets I found has a lot of information that is useful."

"I'm glad of this, Treena."

"Keeliza, these instruments use something we call 'electricity'. It harnesses the power in…" she paused for a minute, realizing they might not understand what she meant.

"It harnesses the power in lightning." She remembered they had talked about that word once during a storm.

"Yes, we know that. You get electricity from the sun, and then use it to power these things."

"Yes."

"We have not chosen to master this."

"Not chosen? I don't understand."

"We discovered this ages past, and chose not to fly that current."

"Why?"

"We knew it was too dangerous. We watched the Hukoovu."

"The Hukoovo used electricity?"

"Yes, and many other things."

"What happened?"

"We will show you and explain. But another day. Today, we have something else to show you."

"What is that, Keeliza?"

"Our child's child's child is to be born today. Wileetu is going to give birth!"

"Your great-grandchild! That is wonderful news!"

Zolweeva said, "Yes, it is. It is a great honor to live to see the third generation."

Trina asked, "That is something I can see?"

Zolweeva answered, "Yes, it is a clan event, and you are part of our clan, now."

Trina didn't know what to say to that, except, "I would be honored."

She climbed on Zolweeva's back, and they flew to another house, where there were many gathered. In the center were two that she'd not met before. One of them, who had a pouch on their back, was crouched on the floor. The other was perched on top of it, with their wings beating.

They had been circumspect about their reproductive processes, so Trina hadn't learned much, and part of it was probably that she was a bit embarrassed to ask. She knew that Zolweeva and Keeliza were mates, and had had children, but she didn't know much more than that. She'd guessed that perhaps Zolweeva was female, because of the pouch, and the meeker demeanor, and Keeliza was male. What was happening at the moment was mysterious to Trina, but she just sat quietly and watched, while the creatures around her were joining together in a soothing, beautiful song.

After about an hour, of this, the one on the top yelled something, and a small, yellowish package that started to wriggle came out. Ah, so now Trina understood what was happening. Wileetu was the one who gave birth, so she must be female. Wileetu got off of her partner and started to lick the small package. It kept moving, and then it buried itself into the pouch. Wileetu's partner's pouch closed over the package, then he stood to his full height.

The rest of the clan surrounded them, and a cacophony of sound started, which then smoothed into harmonious song. Trina just kept sitting and watching. Eventually, individuals started to leave the house, and Trina was left with Zolweeva, Keeliza, Wileetu and her partner, who were busy eating.

Trina said, "I am honored to be welcome here. Congratulations, Wileetu."

Zolweeva translated for her, and Trina noticed that where she'd used nine words, Zolweeva used about fifty, none of which she understood. Keeliza stayed at the house with Wileetu and her partner, and Zolweeva gave Trina a ride back to her own house.

"Zolweeva, do you mind if I ask you some questions?"

"Not at all, Treena. I assumed you would have some. I must go back soon, so if I can't answer all of your questions, we can talk about this another time."

"OK, Zolweeva. Humans have two biological sexes, basically: female and male. Males fertilize eggs inside of females, and females give birth. Females also feed the very young with mammary glands." Trina pointed to her chest. Trina decided that the complexities of sex and gender among humans could wait for a different day.

"I understand. We also have two sexes, like humans. But for us, males are the ones that feed the young with glands that are in the pouch."

Trina said, "That was what I was gathering from what happened today. How long does the young stay in the pouch?"

"About four years until the young learn to fly, but the young will stay close to the male parent to get some nourishment for another three years, or until his partner has another young."

Along with longer days, Johannes also had longer years. Trina remembered reading the report from the probe. Johannes took about 450 days to make its way around its sun.

"How long before the young are fully grown and able to reproduce themselves?"

"About thirty years, but most don't have children until age 40 or so."

"Zolweeva, how old are you?"

"One hundred and twenty years old. I am almost eligible for the elder council."

"How old do you have to be to sit on the elder council?"

"One hundred and fifty."

"How long do most Eeriv live?"

"Some die very young, before they reach one hundred. But most live to 175 or so. Some even make it to 200 years, but that's unusual. There is only one of us in our clan that is that old."

Trina did some quick calculations in her head. Zolweeva had been born around the same time as humans first visited the moon. It was a bit mind-boggling.

"We don't live nearly that long, Zolweeva. Our oldest would live to about seventy-five years. You were born around the time that we were just beginning space travel."

"The Hukoovu are even shorter lived. They only live about forty years."

"Even when they used electricity, and other things?"

"There was a time when they lived longer, yes. But that was a long time ago, and it was a short span of time."

Trina nodded. "Tomorrow, can you show me more about them?"

Zolweeva cooed. "Certainly. But now, I must go back to attend to my... how did you say it?"

"Great-grandchild."

"Yes, my great-grandchild. Tuloosa and Wileetu need a lot of support at this time."

Trina smiled. "I understand. See you tomorrow."

Zolweeva cooed, and then turned and flew out of the house. Trina turned her attention back to the electronics but got distracted by thinking about the differences between the Eeriv, which is what Zolweeva said they called themselves, and humans.

Trina imagined that a species that lived as long as the Eeriv might have a very different attitude toward technological development. She wondered whether that is what explained the fact that they understood far more than they had chosen to put into practice. Humans were almost the opposite, she thought.

The next day, Zolweeva and Keeliza came back to her house in the morning. Trina had just finished her breakfast.

Keeliza said, "Are you ready, Trina?"

"Yes, I am ready."

She climbed onto Zolweeva's back, and they flew out of the house, and above the canopy. They flew over the forest, then across the plains. They passed over the ruins of the colony, which Trina had visited a few more times, to glean supplies and parts. They flew toward the hills in the distance—the direction from which the Hukoovu had come to attack the colony.

Trina could see smoke in the distance. As they approached it, they flew lower down. She could then see dozens of the Hukoovu. Some were sitting by fires, others looked like they were making or building things. Some were tending a pen full of smaller animals. Some were working in fields. Still others were in groups, and looked like they were fighting, or sparring. They kept flying, and flew across a wide river, then across some small hills. Finally, they flew down, and Zolweeva landed on a strange-looking, tall, narrow plateau, one among many set in a regular pattern.

"Where are we?"

Keeliza said, "This is where the Hukoovu used to live."

Trina looked down. The surface on the plateau was made of a kind of moss that looked like it was covering something. She bent down and pulled some of the moss aside. Underneath was smooth, cut stone! It was worn, but it clearly had been built. She looked around again and realized that they were at the top of a building. These strange plateaus were all buildings. She stood and looked around her. She was at the top of a city! She could see the outlines of it, and she could almost imagine what it might have looked like before.

"Can you take me down to the ground, there?" She pointed downward."

Zolweeva said, "No, Treena. There are still Hukoovu that live here, mostly underground. It would be too dangerous for us to go down there."

"How old is this city?"

Keeliza said, "City—is that what you would call it?"

"Yes, we have many cities like this—most larger than this one."

"This is the largest they ever made. It was built about fifty generations ago."

"Fifty of your generations?"

"Yes."

"How did the Hukoovu get from building cities like this, to living as they are now?"

"They ran out of food and metal."

"But they domesticated animals and they farm. Couldn't they have done more of that?"

"The land grew empty from too many crops and animals grazing. It couldn't sustain them."

"Do Eeriv farm?"

"No, that is another thing we have not chosen."

"Because of what happened to the Hukoovu?"

"No, that was a choice made many, many generations ago. The elder council felt that it would create too much separation among us. We didn't want that."

Trina knew that it was easy for the Eeriv to find food—food was abundant in the forest. The only reason the Eeriv would want to farm is if food became scarce. And that would only happen if their population got a lot larger than it was. But that appeared to be something they controlled as well.

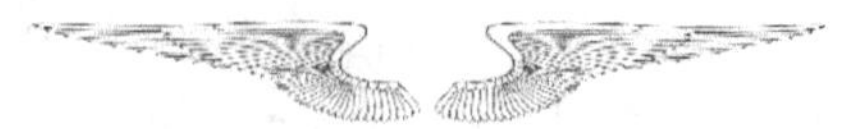

Trina had been busy. She had her hands full with several projects: trying to fix the electronics, setting up her power system for getting maximal solar energy, and getting used to hunting and gathering. Most recently, she'd been busiest with making furniture and comfortable bedding, and she realized she hadn't looked at her tablet in a long time. She wondered what day it was. Sometime in December, she thought.

She turned on the tablet nearest to her, to see that it was Christmas day, 2136. Thirty-four years had passed since that fateful day that her parents died. The Christmas that never was. She didn't even remember Christmas that year. She must have been at LSI that day. For her, only about two years had passed—it seemed almost yesterday for a moment. She thought back on her parents who loved Christmas and tried to make it a special holiday for her and her sister.

She sat on her new couch, which had taken more effort that she thought. She could feel the tears flowing down her face. Here she was, alone on this alien planet, with no family, no companionship, no other human beings. And there would be none for another nine years. She had never been an extrovert, but she was afraid of being so alone.

She heard a coo at her door, and a light tap. She saw Keeliza perched on her porch. She wiped away her tears and got up.

"Keeliza, please come in." Keeliza came in and perched on a perch Trina had made for guests.

"Treena, hello. How are you today?"

Trina said, "I'm sad, Keeliza. Today is a holiday, one my parents enjoyed."

"What kind of holiday?"

"It was to celebrate the birth someone that people revere."

"Ah, we have celebrations like that."

"You do?"

"Yes. In thirty-three days, we celebrate the naming of Gorteeli."

"Who was that?"

"A very wise one, who taught us to avoid the mistakes of the Hukoovu."

"Yeah, sounds wise. So, what do you do?"

"We sing songs, drink special drinks, and we fly far to gather special things for others to eat."

Trina smiled. "That sounds a lot like Christmas."

"Well, perhaps we could help you celebrate? You teach us some songs?"

Trina laughed. "That would be fun!"

"I'll be back in a little while."

Keeliza dropped off of her perch, walked to the porch and flew off. Within just a few minutes, Zolweeva and Litreela had arrived, as well as others she didn't know. And then Keeliza and Weelitu came back carrying clay jars.

Zolweeva said, "You have songs to teach us, Treena?"

Trina said, "Yes! Let's start with Rudolph the Red Nosed Reindeer."

Hearing the Eeriv sing Rudolph the Red Nosed Reindeer was one of the most amazing experiences in her life. She realized that although she was the only human here, her hosts kept treating her as much as possible like one of their own.

The Eeriv had their home trees close to the river, but there was a broad expanse of forest south of where the Eeriv lived. Trina had decided she needed a break from working with the electronics for a while, and went on an adventure, spending a few days away from her home, exploring the forest. It was getting toward evening, and she was beginning to think about stopping for the night.

Ahead of her, she could see that it looked as if the trees were a bit thinner, so she kept walking in that direction, and found a wide clearing. It had the tall grass that was also present in the area where the colony had been, plus some small, odd, rock formations. She walked into the clearing, and found a small boulder, and set her pack down. She'd gathered a fair bit of firewood and she set about making a fire.

As the sun went down, and the flames of the fire danced in front of her, she pondered her current life. She'd been working hard to fix the electronics, make her tree house more like home, and learn as much as she could about Johannes, the Eeriv, and the Hukoovu. She thought about the conversation she'd had with her new friend, Litreela, about the Hukoovu and the trees.

"Are the Hukoovu your enemy?"

"No, I wouldn't call them that, Treena. We try to avoid each other, which is not that hard."

"They've never tried to come into the forest?"

"Not lately. But before they built those big cities, they had wanted to cut down the trees in the forest."

"Really? What did you do?"

"We didn't really do anything."

"I don't understand."

"How much have you learned about the trees, Treena?"

"Well, I know that you revere them, and they sort of, well, do what you ask them to, like make houses."

"We do revere them. They are gracious and give of themselves."

"I know that you don't cut them down. You use limbs and parts of trees that are dead, but you never touch living ones."

"Yes, but the Hukoovu wanted to cut down living trees. The trees did not agree with that."

"What did the trees do? What could they possibly do?"

"The trees, as you have learned, move very slowly. But they do move. And the Hukoovu sleep a lot. They would trap unsuspecting Hukoovu while they slept in the forest."

"Really?"

"Yes. Not many Hukoovu died, but enough so that they never come near the forest anymore."

"Wow. Are the trees intelligent?"

"It depends on how you want to define that. They listen. They speak, if you know their language."

"Do you?"

"No. But some of our clan are trained to listen to them, and speak to them."

Trina could hardly have imagined ending up in a place like this. As the fire died down to embers, she lay down with the blanket under her head, and looked at the stars. Of course, none of the constellations looked the same at all. She had never really seen so many of the stars on Earth, except for when she was in Nevada, but she was mostly too busy to go outside and look up. At home, in Brooklyn, one could never see any stars, and the only way she knew about what constellations looked like was when she'd visited the planetarium as a kid, and in reading about them.

These groups of stars were completely different, although she did know that most of them were visible from Earth, but just in a different arrangement. She wondered which one was Sol. She picked one, imagining it as Sol, imagining a tiny planet circling it, and on that tiny planet was her family. She felt so alone, so far from anything and anyone she cared about. And she knew that no one knew that she was alive, or where she was, and that somehow, felt even worse.

Journal Entry, February 5, 2136

It started to rain yesterday. It was such a surprise, after so many months of sun. It started slowly. There was a wind from the east for a day or so, and then the clouds started, and then rain, and more rain. Zolweeva said that the rain lasts for one hundred and thirty days give or take. I guess winter has come. The Eeriv seem to enjoy the coming of the rain, and it doesn't seem to change their routines at all. I have seen them play in it together, and they fly to and fro as much as they usually do.

I, on the other hand, feel daunted by the intensity of the rain. I've never seen so much water come from the sky. I was soaked within thirty seconds of standing out on my porch. But I have plenty to keep me busy inside. I still haven't finished a few things around the house I want to finish. I'm working on a better way to deal with my toilet, as well as a better way to bathe. The Eeriv groom each other, so they don't bathe, really. And, most importantly, I haven't fixed the narrow-band receiver yet, and I'm determined to get it working.

Last week, I took a trip down to the colony, and set up some memorials for everyone, using scraps of metal, and inscribing names using a tool Keeliza gave me. I was glad to do it - if felt like a kind of closure. My colleagues deserved no less. I even felt some sadness inscribing Sergeant Mason's name.

The loneliness comes and goes. Some days it feels almost crippling, other days, I hardly notice it, being busy with all that I am doing. Zolweeva and Keeliza, in particular, are around a lot, although I'm also becoming good friends with Litreela, a young male, who hasn't found a mate yet. He learned English fast and likes to ask me a lot of questions about human history.

I am still frustrated by what feels like the impossibility of learning their language. Litreela is giving me some lessons, and I'm learning slowly, but I fear he thinks me stupid, which, frankly, compared to them, I probably am. And I know that I will never really understand them until I can learn their language.

Signals from Earth: March 2136

Finally, after many weeks of working on it, she got the narrow-band receiver to work. The video stream started immediately when she turned the device on. At first, she couldn't figure out what was playing. It seemed to be some sort of parade, except it was very grim-looking.

"Today, in Times Square, we celebrate the sixth anniversary of the New Order. The President is presiding over the parade."

Trina looked at the president, and he looked very familiar to her, but she couldn't place him. Must be some politician she'd seen when she was a kid. The datestamp on the video feed was July 24, 2130, six years ago.

"Welcome to NON News. I'm Peter Trilling. Today, President Sarchet declared this day a holiday, to forever commemorate the day that the United States released itself from the blasphemous tyranny of the World Government."

World Government? When Trina had left, things had certainly been moving quickly in that direction, but it seemed surprising to her that in such a short space of time, there could have been a world government that had already dissolved? Or perhaps only the US withdrew?

"President Sarchet has also said that the United States is declaring all treaties signed with other countries to be null and void. 'The United States will go its own way, forge its own path into the future, and live by its Christian values. We know that God is with us, and only God can save us.'"

"In other news, the New Order has moved everyone in New York City out of harm's way, after the last minor storm. Because of flooding due to the storm, the entire city is now under water, and people have been moved to safety in upstate New York."

Minor storm causing flooding? This seemed really strange. And the president's name seemed so familiar to her, but no matter how hard she tried, she couldn't figure out where she'd heard it before.

"In more news, residents of a small town in Kansas have been finally rescued, after hiding in their shelter when a tornado touched down in Hodgeman County, Kansas. The President himself will honor these plucky survivors in a ceremony at the White House tomorrow morning."

Trina connected the video feed output into one of the tablets, which she figured out could record several days of video. She would have to spend time skimming it, to see if she could understand some of what had happened. So much of what was said didn't make much sense to her. She'd missed a lot—but it was hard for her to think that so much could have happened in so little time.

She remembered the briefing about communications, and how Kepler Exploratory would send news and events through this feed, in perpetuity. So far, she'd seen nothing of news of any of the other ships that had been sent to other places. She assumed that some news of the first colony had been sent back to Kepler Exploratory by the communications group in her colony, before the disaster struck. She realized that news wouldn't make it back to Earth for another 7 years. It was likely that the third ship to follow would eventually get that news as well.

The problem was, they wouldn't have the right information. Well, that was Trina's job—to make sure that when they arrived, she would be there to fill them in completely, to prevent it from happening a third time.

She left the receiver and decided to get something to eat. After being here for more than 100 days, Trina began to feel it was time to pull her own weight and stop accepting all of the gifts of food. She asked Zolweeva to explain to here where they got their food from, and it took a while before Zolweeva understood Trina's perspective. The Eeriv didn't feel in any way resentful of her or helping her get food— they really wanted to help her, and she knew they would for as long as she lived. But she wanted to learn for herself, so that she could teach the others when they came.

She'd done testing on all of the food she'd been given, and, as she remembered hearing from others, there were missing essential amino acids, particularly Valine, Leucine and Isoleucine. She knew her body could not produce them, and they were completely missing from the chemistry of the planet. She found enough supplements to last her about thirty years. So, she depended on the arrival of the new colony, with its own supplements, and, finally, ways to produce the amino acids for everyone.

Zolweeva had shown her the fish-like animals they got from the river, and he also showed her about twenty plants that were edible for the Eeriv. They of course, simply swooped down from the sky and caught the fish, but Trina had to painstakingly build a boat, then some nets to catch them. They were large, more than forty pounds, and Trina learned to smoke the meat in her clay oven. But she generally gave her leftovers to Zolweeva and Keeliza, who graciously took them.

She'd fish about once a week, and she'd gather edible plants several times a week. It felt satisfying to her to do this—it got her out of her head. She liked walking along the forest's floor, noticing what was there, and learning about the different plants and animals, carefully cataloging them. The Eeriv spent most of their time either in the trees, or on the forest's edge near the river. Trina actually taught Zolweeva some things about the forest floor, where he'd never been before. She often took camping trips deep into the forest.

Today, she was experimenting with a plant that, from her analysis, had nothing poisonous in it, although the Eeriv didn't eat it. It was delicious to Trina's taste, and nothing bad had come of her tasting it a few days ago. Today, she would try to sauté it in some of the fish-fat that she'd learned how to separate.

She heard a coo from the porch, and she walked out of the kitchen to the main room, to see Litreela perched on the porch. Litreela was Zolweeva's youngest grandchild, the uncle to the newest in the family. She and Litreela had begun to get to know one another. Where Zolweeva was curious about human language, Litreela was curious about human history. He was writing a book about it, with Trina's help, of course.

"The setting sun / yellow-green in the west sky / tilts wings gives warmth as / am warm in seeing face / reflect great wide light west, Litreela," Trina said the standard afternoon greeting in the language of the Eeriv that Litreela had painstakingly taught Trina.

"Good Afternoon, Treena," Litreela replied in English.

"I thought we were getting together tomorrow."

"We are, Treena. But I have one question, I hope you don't mind."

"Not at all. Do you mind if I bring out my lunch? Are you hungry?"

"I just ate, thank you. Please, bring your lunch."

Trina went back in the kitchen, finished cooking her food, and came out with the plate, and a cup of water. She sat down in her chair, across from the perching Litreela.

"So, what's the question?"

"I was thinking about yesterday's conversation about what you called 'war.'"

"And?"

"I'm trying to understand what would cause one clan to fight another."

"Well, Litreela, what if there were another group of Eeriv on the other side of the forest, and for some reason, there were fewer kleeza to eat?"

"Well, we would meet together, and decide who would move."

"And what if neither clan wanted to move."

"What do you mean, Treena? Both clans would want to move."

"Why would both clans want to move?"

"They would get great honor for taking on that task of moving themselves for the sake of both clans."

Trina realized in that moment that it would be very difficult to make Litreela, or any Eeriv, understand war.

"OK, what about this—what would happen if the Hukoovu invaded the forest?"

"They would never do that! You know, they are afraid of the forest, and the trees trap them."

"But what if they somehow over their fear, and avoided being trapped by the trees? What would you do?"

"Well, I don't think we would do anything. They can't climb trees, and so they couldn't really bother us."

"What if they found the river, and started eating all of the kleeza?"

Litreela was silent for a moment. "Well, then we would move, and we would know our own honor, even if the Hukoovu did not."

Trina sighed, and said, "Is there anything you can think of, Litreela, which would cause you to fight?"

"Fight? You mean, like injure or kill other Eeriv?"

"Yes."

Litreela was silent again, this time for a long time.

"No, Treena, I'm sorry. I can't think of anything."

"Well, this is why you can't understand war. Humans will fight over almost anything. They will fight to protect resources, like food or water. They will fight to protect land, and fight to protect ideology."

"Ideology? What is that?"

"It's a particular point of view—when some people decide that their point of view is the right one, and all the other ones are wrong."

"But how could anyone decide that Treena? Everyone must know that many points of view can be right at the same time."

Trina could not help but laugh, but when she saw the look on Litreela's face, she stopped. She was getting good at recognizing Eeriv emotions, and there was shame on Litreela's face. "Litreela, don't worry—you are correct, and many humans are incorrect. Many humans don't understand that."

"I see." The shame was gone, replaced by a perplexed look. "I will go now, Treena, and think about what you have told me, and write some more. Human beings are very different than Eeriv, aren't they?"

Trina smiled. "Yes, we are very different. I wish sometimes we were a lot more like you."

"You seem to be like us, Treena. You are part of our clan, now."

"I am honored to be a part of your clan, Litreela. I hope that I may someday earn that honor."

Litreela cooed, then hopped off the perch, walked onto the porch, and flew away, leaving Trina to finish her lunch, and think. She began to think of the little she'd seen of the transmissions from Earth and wondered if the New Order were a new kind of ideology. That scared her. When large groups of human beings adopted big, new ideologies, nothing but war and destruction followed.

New Beginnings: May 2136

Treena had now pieced together what had happened on Earth. It was a challenge, given the lopsided nature of the broadcasts, but she thought she could read through the lines some. She'd recorded about five days' worth of broadcasts, as well as listened to many hours that she'd not recorded.

First, it seemed that Kepler Exploratory was no more. The broadcasts took two forms. The first were clearly propaganda shows that were shown to people in the United States. Then, about once a week, there were broadcasts that were clearly meant for the colonies, the fate of which those on Earth did not know, at least not at the time of these broadcasts.

It seemed that about twenty-five years ago, about five years after they had left, a world government, led by the US and Europe, had formed, and that government had almost immediately put into place massive measures to stop the climate disaster that had already decimated the planet. Then, a charismatic character arose in US politics, against world government, and had managed to sway the country to leave the world government. When that happened, the world government predictably collapsed, leading to at least three different wars.

In the meantime, global climate change was getting far worse than it had been, rendering hundreds of thousands of square miles uninhabitable, due to either the encroaching sea, horrible drought, or too high temperatures. The government seemed to be mostly engaged in moving people to safety, but it was not engaged in any effort to change the situation.

It did appear that the last ship got away before the collapse of the world government. She could tell that the current government did not care what had happened to the colonists but seemed proud of their accomplishments in the Solar System. That seemed somewhat irrelevant given how horrible the situation on the ground was, but the broadcasts spend quite a bit of time covering it.

It was a surprise when she learned that CalSpace had become the "Government's Official Space Company." She wondered what that meant, and what had happened. When she was part of it, CalSpace only did tourism.

She thought about her sister, who would have been about thirty-nine when these broadcasts were made and would be about forty-five now. Trina wondered how she was, having been moved from New York City up to upstate NY. It was unclear what the conditions for those people were like. The broadcasts showed people who said they were happy but showed nothing about how they were living. She hoped her sister was doing alright, and wished she had a way to make contact with her. But even if she did have a transmitter, there was no way to get a message to her sister.

The third colony ship was about three-quarters through its trip to Kepler 75f. She wondered whether or not the awake crew were listening to these transmissions. She decided she'd learned about all she was going to learn for a while, so she turned off the receiver and recorder, and set about her other big task: learning the Eeriv language, both written and spoken.

It was so very different than English. Some things were not surprising—the Eeriv language had many, many words for concepts like 'honor' and 'love' and 'joy'. They had many words for the sky, and for clouds. Since they flew, instead of walked, their idioms were so different than hers. And sentences had so many more words. Where English had words in the couple of hundred thousand realm, Litreela told her that they actively used over two million words.

The hard part for Trina was that parts of speech were so different, and differently used. The closest analogs to adjectives and adverbs were much more central to the formation of sentences than the noun and verb analogs. Where in English the sentence "I ate" was enough to give a lot of information, in Eeriv, it would not have been enough to simply use just a pronoun and a verb. That would be a sentence fragment that would not carry any meaning. Often, sentences in Eeriv had no verbs, which Trina found confusing. A sentence like, "That wonderful easy kleeza in my belly," would have more meaning to them than "I ate."

Trina knew that she would never be fluent in Eeriv, even though some of them were already fluent in English. She thought it was a good thing that so many could become fluent in English, as it would be important to build relationships between the colony that was coming and the Eeriv.

The new colony made her nervous, even though it was a long time away. She didn't know what they would be like. Some members of her colony, like Security, were not very nice, and she could imagine problems with the Eeriv. But she hoped that they could bridge their differences, especially since the Eeriv would know so much about humans before they got here.

Journal Entry, August 10, 2140

It's my birthday, today. It is my twenty-fifth birthday, even though I was born fifty-five years ago. It's hard to believe that my parents died thirty-eight years ago. I'm sure my grandparents are long dead. I hope my little sister and cousins are having a decent life, although from what I can tell from the few broadcasts I watch, I doubt it.

Life on Earth seems to be on a downward spiral. The transmissions that I have looked at lately seem to suggest that food is running out, there are a lot of wars happening, and climate change has continued unabated, making for terrible storms, and rendering so much of the world impossible to live in.

For many reasons, I'm glad I'm not there. I do still sometimes wish my parents were alive, and I do get lonely, still, but my life here has been good. I've been on Johannes now for four years. I understand more and more Eeriv language, and Litreela keeps teaching me. The other day, he excitedly said that I'm talking at the same level as his newest niece, who turned two the other day. I know he sees that as a compliment, but I couldn't help but hearing "you talk like an infant," when he said it.

Litreela and I had the closest thing to an argument the other day. I had noticed that all of the other Eeriv his age had already found mates. The Eeriv are like birds on Earth. They choose a mate early in life and stick to that mate for their entire lives. Many Eeriv travel between clans to find mates, some find mates within their own clan.

I asked Litreela when he was going to choose a mate, and he told me that he had chosen not to be mated. I'd never heard of that, so I asked him why. He explained that he had chosen to spend his time with me, learning about me, and humans, and that he would stay with me. He felt that choosing a mate would mean that he couldn't spend the time with me that he wanted to. He said he had the blessing of the clan.

I didn't know what to say at first. I said that of course, it was his choice, but I felt that maybe he'd be missing out on something, and that he should re-think it. He was insulted, which then I had to explain that I didn't mean to insult him, I just wanted him to do what's best for him. He explained that spending time with me was best for him.

Litreela and I have spent countless hours together. We've flown far, talked about everything. I know that I love him, but it still feels strange that he's chosen my companionship over that of an Eeriv mate.

The Ocean: September 2141

Trina heard a rustle in the trees above her and looked up to see Litreela about twenty feet up on a branch, peering down at her. She was about half-way between the east end of the clearing with the old colony and the river, and about two hours walk to her tree. She had been spending the last few days breaking a trail between the clearing and the river.

First, she wanted the trail. Although Litreela and other Eeriv would fly her wherever she wanted to go, she wanted to move in the forest, and between the old colony and the river on her own. Second, she thought that since the next colony would have to move, probably to the forest, why not have a trail cut already for them to follow?

She didn't know anything about building a trail, and of course the Eeriv, who spent virtually no time on the ground, could not be very helpful. She did the best she could. Marking trees with paint, moving rocks and debris, and just choosing the best places for the trail to go. She had already noticed since the last time she was here that the trail was wider than it had been before. The trees were moving out of the way. It was hard for her to get used to that. But she certainly was glad that they weren't doing the reverse, which they certainly could choose to.

"Treena," Litreela called, then cooed.

"Hi Litreela."

"What are you doing?"

"I told you—I'm making a trail to walk between the clearing and the river."

"But I would carry you anywhere."

"I know that Litreela. But I like to walk, and other humans like to walk. It's good for us to walk. We evolved this way. Besides, when the new colony comes, they can't all be dependent on you. So, I'm making these trails."

"I understand. Are we still going to the ocean tomorrow?"

Trina smiled. "Yes! I can pick this back up when we get back."

Litreela cooed, then flew off, and Trina continued digging up the big rock that was currently in the middle of the trail. When she had successfully dug it up and pushed it way to the side, she decided to call it quits for the day, and walk home.

She never got tired of the forest. She loved exploring it, finding new plants and animals to add to her catalog. Any new plants she'd not seen before, she'd take a sample, to determine whether or not it might be edible. So far, she'd found over thirty plants that she could eat, many of which were poisonous to Eeriv, but harmless to her. In most cases, they were quite delicious.

One particular plant made large violet berries, larger than grapes. She dubbed the plant the "violetberry bush." One berry could kill an Eeriv, but they were completely harmless to her. They tasted like something between a tart raspberry and a cranberry. She liked tart things.

She arrived at her tree, and she did her standard inspection of things when she arrived at it from the ground. She'd built a pretty deep septic system, which seemed to be doing well. Eeriv just eliminated on the fly, but since there weren't very many of them, it seemed not to overwhelm the forest in any way, and the trees probably appreciated the fertilizer. She knew that she'd have to learn how to deal with her own waste, given that she did not know how human waste would affect the forest environment. Eventually, when the new colony arrived, they would have to build more of these.

She climbed up her tree, entered into the door that she'd had to get made on one side, so she could actually get into her house. The porch entrance was difficult to climb around.

She remembered the day that one Eeriv arrived who was, in her translation, a "tree whisperer." He would touch and stroke the tree where she wanted the door, and then he placed a very small stone in the wall. He would replace the stone with larger ones, step by step. Then, he started to place a frame around the growing hole, and eventually there was a door. It was as if he was just telling the tree where he wanted the door, and the tree complied with his request. It took a couple of hours, but she understood more about the Eeriv and the trees during that time than she'd learned in years.

The next day, she woke up to the sun streaming into her room. Today was a special day. Once in a while, Litreela would take her on long flying trips. Today, they were starting a trip to the ocean that would take several days. Keeliza and Zolweeva were coming as well. She went to finish packing what she'd need for the trip. She had a change of clothing, some extra food, as well as some instrumentation—she wanted to learn about the composition of the ocean.

Litreela had originally said that there was only one ocean, but Trina had shown him the maps of the planet that the probe had made, and he had been astonished. The planet was not mostly ocean, like Earth, but it was about 40% ocean, with three oceans each smaller than Earth's smallest ocean.

Trina heard a coo outside her door, and she grabbed her pack, and walked out on the porch, to see Litreela perched on it.

"Greetings / the bright light shines / the new eastern sun warms /gladness of heart / your face is, Litreela," Trina greeted him speaking Eeriv.

He replied, also in Eeriv, "The new dawn / bright lovely warmth / eyes and heart sing, Treena. My pouch / light comfort settle / this great trip. Zolweeva heavy light / weakness in bones / sad not to honor / flight this grand sweeping / far travel adventure."

Trina nodded and switched to English. "I'm so sorry to hear that, Litreela. I hope he gets better."

"He will, Treena. Keeliza is tending him. Tuloosa and Wileetu would like to come with us. Is this alright?"

Trina said in Eeriv, "Honored and glad / seeing presence, wings / superb, meritorious flight." Eh, she thought, not well said. But Litreela didn't seem to mind. None of them ever did. Sometimes they would gently correct her, or give her advice, but mostly they seemed happy that she even tried.

She put on her pack and climbed into Litreela's pouch. Litreela took off, and went up above the canopy, where Tuloosa and Wileetu were waiting perched near one of the platforms. As they approached, Trina could see the small head of their second child poking out of Tuloosa's pouch.

They all shared greetings, mostly in Eeriv, since Tuloosa and Wileetu were not fluent in English.

Trina knew that this child didn't have a name—they chose their own names, when the time came, when they reached their first majority, at age twenty-five. Developmentally, this was quite similar to the human age of sixteen, although the Eeriv could not reproduce yet, that wouldn't happen for another five to ten years. That was called their second majority, and that is around when they would choose a mate.

Their first child, the one that Trina had seen born, had learned to fly, but wasn't quite ready for a trip of this kind, so she was with friends, who had a child of their own that was about a year younger.

Litreela said to Trina, in English, "Shall we go now?"

Trina nodded, and he took off. Trina always loved these trips. She'd only ever flown in a plane once, but here, she flew all of the time. She got to know the land best while she was on the back of this or that Eeriv. They loved to fly her places, and she loved being flown. Litreela flew her around the most.

Litreela had said that the trip to the ocean would take about a day and a half each way. So she knew she would be flying over land she'd never seen before. She had a camera, as well as recording binoculars, and she used them at intervals while they flew. They followed the river. Eventually, the forest opened up into a wide-open valley, which was green, and dotted by trees. The valley continued like this until they stopped for the evening in a copse of smallish trees next to the river.

When they stopped, Trina asked Litreela, "Do the Hukoovu ever come here?"

"No, Treena. They would have to travel through the forest to get here because of the cliffs to the north, and they never go near the forest."

The Eeriv spent almost no time on the ground. The five of them, with Trina, landed on the top of the trees. They shared a meal, and then Trina climbed down the tree. These particular trees were not very tall, and they were definitely not amenable to her sleeping in them. She laid out her sleeping bag and pillow and went promptly to sleep.

She was awoken by a cold feeling on her neck. She opened her eyes to see the little one, who was out of the pouch, trying to make its way into her sleeping bag! She looked up to see Tuloosa perched on a rock nearby. She imagined this was meant as her wake up call, but she wasn't really inclined to rise at that moment. She opened the bag, and let the little one in. He curled up next to her chest and fell asleep. She felt very honored that Tuloosa trusted her so much.

After a while, Tuloosa came closer, and started to coo. The little one woke up, and crawled out of Trina's sleeping bag, and went back into Tuloosa's pouch.

"Greetings / bright light of new eastern sun / glad heart to awake / your face, Tuloosa. Honor mine / your smallest / lie quiet inside my pouch."

"Greetings the new dawn / bright lovely warmth, Treena. Honor great gladness / smallest finds your pouch light / love bright comfort."

Trina got out of her sleeping bag, and had a small bite to eat, packed up, then climbed back up the tree, where Litreela, Tuloosa, and Wileetu were perched.

Litreela said, "Ready to go, Treena?"

Trina nodded and climbed onto Litreela. They flew again, still following the river. Occasionally, Trina would see other flying creatures, smaller than the Eeriv. They seemed wary of the Eeriv. She also spotted some large-ish animals that looked a lot like deer or antelope, also with six limbs. She wondered how the probe missed these—she thought that it had only found evidence of much smaller animals. The trees became fewer and smaller, and eventually there were only bushes and a kind of tall grass. Eventually, Trina could see sand dunes, and finally, the ocean.

Trina had only been to the ocean once, when she was a small child, and her family took a trip out to Idywild Park Beach one day. There had been a lot of abandoned housing right near the beach, as well as some buildings emerging from the surf now and then. Here, everything was completely pristine. She could see the wide swath of the river as it joined the ocean.

They stopped on the top of a sand dune, and Trina got off Litreela, and walked down to the edge of the ocean. She opened her pack and took out her sample containers. She took a couple of jars full of water, and one with a bit of sand from the bottom. She then sat down, and watched the water move in and out slowly. There were a few waves, but not many, and they weren't very big.

Johannes didn't have a moon, so Trina knew that there would be no tides. She imagined that the infrequent storms might cause the waves to get higher at times, but that probably, the shoreline had looked like this for eons. It was peaceful, and quite pleasant. The smells were different than she was used to. There was a kind of pungency in the air, as well as some sweetness. She didn't know whether that was the water, or some plant life nearby.

"Litreela, how often do the Eeriv visit the ocean?"

"I've been here only once before. Most Eeriv don't fly further away from home than they can do in one day."

Trina nodded. There were a few Eeriv whose job it was to ferry communications between the clans—the nearest clan was about one day's flight away. Generally, the clans lived fairly far apart from each other, but any news would reach another clan within a day.

Trina noticed Tuloosa and Wileetu's young one testing the water: moving in, then scurrying away when the wave came in. Trina recorded it on her camera—it was very cute. She got up, and walked along the shore for a while, but the landscape was the same for as far as she could see. She would remember to look at the probe images of the ocean and the shore to get an idea of what the shoreline looked like from above.

After about an hour, she signaled that she was ready to leave. She had been tempted to take a swim, but she didn't want to risk it before analyzing the water. She climbed onto Litreela's back, and they headed back to their past evening's campground to spend the night.

When they returned home, Trina bid Litreela and the others good night. She was tired, but not sleepy, so Trina turned on the receiver, mostly out of curiosity. She didn't tune in all that often these days. Mostly, it was just depressing.

She looked at the display, and braced herself for more propaganda, telling how well the New Order are doing things, and how much the US was prospering and growing. Even though it was clearly evident from the other broadcasts that the US, and the whole world, was struggling.

But there was nothing on the air. Nothing at all. A screen full of snow. Trina decided to write a quick program to have her tablet alert her when the signal changed. She didn't know if that would ever happen, but if it did, she knew she would want to see it.

A few days later, her tablet sounded an alert. She turned on the video, to see a straggly-haired man sitting in ramshackle room, Trina knew this was not going to be a standard broadcast.

"Hello. My name is Everett Colden. I was a scientist who worked for Kepler Exploratory. A group of us have been trying to take over the equipment seized by the New Order, allowing us to communicate with you. We finally have the equipment and brought it to safety. We don't know how long we'll have power to transmit, but as long as we do, we'll broadcast at least once daily, at 12:00 noon local time.

"We have now gotten transmissions from most of the ships. The first mission to Kepler 75f found that it was not habitable, and they went on to Kepler 89a. We heard back from the first colony, then the second, which said the first had been destroyed. However, messages from the second colony stopped abruptly, and we have not heard from them in weeks. We have also heard from the third ship, which is still in transit to Kepler 89a. They changed course to go directly there, instead of stopping at 75f."

Trina was glad to hear that the ship was definitely on its way. She thought that meant that they might be here a little sooner than expected, although not much sooner. A direct line from Earth to Johannes wasn't all that much shorter than the line through 75f.

"The first ship sent to 57d found it not habitable, and they went then to 58c. That planet wasn't habitable either, and that ship did not have any more fuel to make it further. The second ship originally slated to go to 57d changed course to go directly to try Kepler 86g, but they have not been heard from. The third ship went directly to 86g, and they are on route.

"All three missions to Kepler 65g are present on the planet, and they are surviving. It is a somewhat forbidding climate. A very cold planet, with water ice covering the ocean over most of the northernmost and southernmost parts of the planet. The lower temperate and tropical zones are mostly open ocean except for island archipelagos, most of which have a climate similar to northern Canada. Those colonists are doing alright and have even begun to raise some of the animals they brought with them."

Trina thought that made tons of sense. Start raising sheep, goats, reindeer, and other hardy animals for food and labor. It would be tough going, and hopefully there are creatures in the oceans that are edible, and they can grow some food crops in greenhouses.

"I don't know who is listening to these broadcasts. I assume that colonies on 65g are, and I hope that other colonists are watching as well. I need to give you a detailed update on how things stand right now on Earth.

"As you probably surmised by now, Kepler Exploratory is no more. It was taken over, like all corporations, by the government of the New Order. The New Order is a totalitarian, Christian regime that has murdered millions because they would not conform to the ideals of the regime. They have ignored climate change, which is devastating the planet. Temperatures continue to climb. Ten years ago was the last winter where the arctic had any ice, every single glacier is melted now, and Antarctica is now snow-free for all but the deepest part of winter. Many people have fled from Australia and most areas of the Middle East and Africa, which have become largely uninhabitable, sometimes with temperatures up to one hundred and sixty in the summertime. The sea levels have gone so high that every city that had been on the ocean is now underwater, including Amsterdam, Shanghai, New York, LA, San Francisco, and many others. Last year saw the end of Indonesia and a number of other island nations. The central valley of California is now a sea. Food is scarce, and people are dying of starvation and disease.

"Luckily, the New Order is crumbling, and in some places, small, local governments have taken over, and are doing good things. I'm broadcasting from a small town in Washington State, called Wenatchee. Most of the northwest part of the US is out of New Order control, and they are working on putting together some sort of larger government in this area. We have hope that we'll be able to get ourselves back on our feet. The northwest has plenty of arable land, and not too many people."

"We need to preserve power. We'll be back tomorrow. We want to encourage messages from colonies. We know it will take years for messages to come to us, then go out to the other colonies, but it would be good if you all are in some semblance of contact with each other, and with Earth."

The signal cut off, and there was nothing left. Trina set her tablet to record each day at this time, Earth time. She was glad to hear that there was at least one colony that was doing well, and she hoped that it would be two, once the third ship arrived. She felt like she had a lot to do.

Next Ship: January 2143

Trina returned from one of her trips to the valley beyond the forest. It had been a good trip. Some of the crops that she'd planted had sprouted and grown. Others hadn't, and she didn't quite know why, but she'd try something different with those.

She turned on one of tablets and looked at the calendar. It was January 5, 2143. It turned out that there had been a recorded transmission from yesterday. The transmissions from Earth had gotten less and less frequent, and finally, they had signed off for the foreseeable future because they had no source of power. They promised to do their best, but it had been more than a year since she'd seen a transmission.

She started to play the recording and she was greeted with the face of a man who looked to be in a very small room. She turned up the volume.

"Hello, there. Everything is going well here on the *Calypso*. The captain is now awake again and beginning the preparations for arrival at Johannes. No transmissions from Johannes have been received since 2135, so we're not even sure that anyone is hearing this message. But we're doing this anyway. We'll be updating you, whoever you are, if you exist, on our landing place, and time. Ship is on target for arrival at Kepler 89a in orbit on January 8, 2145, three years from now. We can't use too much energy to transmit very often. Signing off for now, more tomorrow."

She set the tablet to record the messages from *Calypso*. She now had a date certain for the arrival of the new colony. It was still some time away, but there was still much to do. She had been preparing for this for eight years. Over the last eight years, things had been easy. She'd learned how to hunt and gather, and what she could and couldn't eat. She'd learned how to build her own furniture and had been able to gather enough things she needed from the ruins of the old colony, like clothing, supplements, and varied equipment. She'd gotten older, and she thought wiser, but she missed other human beings. She did have plenty of good friends among the Eeriv and was an honored member of the clan. There were already seven books written about humans, and Eeriv from all over would come to visit her.

They knew that a new colony of humans would come, and she had hope that there could be friendship. But she had also warned her friends that not all humans were always friendly, especially when threatened.

She now knew where they should land, but of course she had no way of telling them that. If they decided to land somewhere far away from the Hukoovu, then she wouldn't have to be in a position to try and tell them that they would have to move. But if they landed right where the first two colonies landed, which, she realized, was probably the most likely, she would need to meet them before they did any significant work setting up.

Journal Entry, December 25, 2143

It is my ninth Christmas here. After the first Christmas, where I taught the Eeriv Christmas carols, I've been celebrating more quietly. Litreela asked me about this a few years ago, and I explained that I wanted to wait until I there were more humans here before I celebrated in the way I used to.

I think he understood. As much different as the Eeriv are to us, we have very similar emotions. It seems that at least Litreela and I can understand each other on those terms, even though our minds work very differently.

I don't dream about my family very often anymore, but last night I had a very vivid dream about my sister. I was walking down a road, and I saw this middle-aged woman and a younger woman walking ahead of me. The middle-aged woman looked so familiar. I ran to catch up, and the woman opened her mouth with surprise.

"Trina? It's Mita!"

"Mita!"

We hugged. Mita introduced me to her daughter, who she'd named after me. I was so touched. I told her she looked just like Mom. She told me that I looked just the same as I did when I left. She asked me how that was possible. I told her I'd been asleep for 33 years.

She said that she wanted me to meet all of the family. Bettina and Theresa's children and grandchildren, and her own grandchildren.

"We live in a small house, but it's alright."

But then, I was dragged by some sort of wind away from them, and they were shouting and screaming for me to come back, and then I woke up. I felt both happy and sad. Happy to see Mita, and sad that I could not stay.

I wonder almost every day how my family is. And I wish that somehow, they could know where I am, and that I'm alright. Maybe someday, when the new colony comes, I can attach a message to go to Mita, and somehow, maybe somehow, she'll get it.

The work of preparation for the new colony continues. I'd gleaned a big store of seeds from the wreckage of the old colony, and I've done test planting on the edge of the valley. I'm not an agronomist. I did the best I could. We'll see what happens when I visit next. Perhaps there will be some plants waiting for me.

Arrival: January 2145

Today was the day she'd been waiting for for 10 Earth years, or 3000 Johannes days. The new colony ship would be sending a shuttle down to the same place where the first and second colony landed. Predictable, but unfortunate. Trina would have to try and convince them that they would have to move.

Luckily, she'd prepared recordings of the Hukoovu that she'd taken while flying over them with Litreela one day. But she was wary. She had no idea whether or not they would be friendly to her, and to the Eeriv.

Zolweeva, Keeliza, Litreela and Trina had talked for hours a few days ago about whether or not they should accompany her to meet the new colony. They were eager to meet new humans, and make friends, and Trina felt that it would be important to have the humans understand right off the bat that there were two other intelligent species on Johannes, one friendly, and one not.

Trina eventually agreed to let Zolweeva and Litreela accompany her, but she was worried. She didn't know how the new colonists would react to them and react to her presence as the sole survivor. She cautioned both of them and made them promise that they would fly away and leave her when she told them to.

One of the improvements she'd made to her house was to fashion a solar hot water heater and shower. She got into her shower, and pulled the lever that would let the hot water in. She had about 2 minutes of hot water, and she took full advantage of it. Over the years, she had grown out her dreadlocks again, and she washed them well.

The Eeriv didn't have soap. They groomed themselves and each other, so they had no need of washing. They washed their earthenware with sand and rinsed it with water. She had tried various kinds of methods for soap-making and had finally found a nice recipe that worked with the fat of the fish-like animal from the river, and other materials she could find, or the Eeriv could provide. It smelled quite nice, from her perspective.

She got out of the shower, dried herself off, and dressed. She packed a tablet she'd prepared, some food and water, and some assorted supplies in a backpack. She walked out onto her porch, and Zolweeva and Litreela had just arrived.

"Momentous grand occasion / awaits Treena readiness / nervousness body?" Zolweeva asked in Eeriv.

Trina replied in English, "I'm as ready as I will ever be Zolweeva. Are you?"

Zolweeva said in English, "Yes, Treena, we are ready."

Trina climbed onto Litreela's back, as Zolweeva had become too weak to carry her. They flew to the edge of the forest and sat high in the trees. Trina took out her binoculars. They would wait at the edge of the forest, until the shuttle landed, and people started to disembark to set up the first camp.

In a couple of hours, Zolweeva said, "Treena, look above!"

Trina looked, and could see a shuttle, with its contrail behind it, moving in the sky over their location. She watched in her binoculars as the shuttle flew over, and then dropped down quite close to the remains of the second colony.

Trina said, "OK, let's go."

Soon would be the moment Trina had been waiting for. It had been a long time since she'd seen another human being. She hadn't even seen herself except for reflections in the river, since the Eeriv didn't have mirrors.

They flew from the trees toward the camp. As they approached, Litreela said, "Treena, where should we land?"

Trina looked could see that they had started to disembark, and several people were hauling out containers from the shuttle. One of those on the ground looked up, and shouted, and many people started to point.

She said to Litreela, "Over there, where there are fewer people. They have already seen us anyway."

They landed, and the crew from the ship stood back. Trina got off of Litreela's back and walked toward them. One man, who looked like he was probably in charge, came up to her.

Trina said, "Hi. I know this looks surprising."

He said, "And who are you?"

"I'm Trina Dewing, sole survivor of the second colony. This is Zolweeva, and Litreela."

The man said, "I'm Commander Ellery Rincón, First Officer of the *Calypso*."

Trina said, "Nice to meet you, Commander. I have some important news to tell you. You need to move the colony. Both the first and second colonies were destroyed by a species that the Eeriv, my friends here, call the 'Hukoovu.' This is part of their territory. They are very, very large, and they eat meat. There is some very nice land on the other side of the forest that will be a great place for a new colony."

Commander Rincón said, "And how did you survive the attack? It's been 10 years."

"I climbed a tree to escape them. Zolweeva rescued me." She pointed to him. "There are plants and animals that are edible for humans, as long as you take supplements, which I gleaned from the wreckage of the second colony. I've been living with the Eeriv for all of this time. They are very intelligent, and gracious hosts."

By now, all of the people from the shuttle were gathered around the Commander. One man whispered into the Commander's ear. Trina recognized the uniform—he was Security. She wondered what it was he was telling the Commander, as his face changed from friendly to confused.

Zolweeva moved forward a little and said, in English, "The Eeriv wish to welcome you to the planet you have named Johannes. We hope that we can provide you with whatever you need."

Clearly, none of them expected Zolweeva to speak, let alone speak English. It silenced the background chatter, and then there was murmuring from the assembled people.

A woman with striking green eyes and brown hair, standing a few feet from the Commander, came forward and said, "They speak English?"

Trina said, "Yes. They learned English a lot faster than I could learn their language. They have a much better command of language than I do, and their language is very complicated. I have been learning it for all this time, and I speak it about as well as one of their infants."

She asked, "Are the… the 'Hukoovu' intelligent?"

"Yes, they are. They are very different than the Eeriv, but they are also intelligent."

"So, there are two intelligent species here? How did the probes miss that?"

"The Hukoovu used to be technological, but they lost that many generations ago. The Eeriv decided not to embrace technology, so there wasn't really anything for the probe to find."

The man in the security uniform was getting agitated, and three more Security officers were now at the front.

The Commander said, "Ms. Dewing, Security has informed me that you are the prime suspect for the sabotage of the second colony.

"What? I don't understand."

The officer that had been whispering to the Commander strode forward.

"You were reported by Security of the *Precious Hope* to be a suspected saboteur. Now that it appears that colony is no more, and you are the only survivor, it would seem obvious that you would be a suspect."

Trina said, "But neither colony was a victim of sabotage! They were both destroyed by the Hukoovu!"

"And I am to believe a suspected saboteur and sole survivor?"

"Look, I have recordings I took of them—you can see them for yourselves!"

"Recordings can be faked. You've had 10 years to fake them."

Litreela said, "Treena is faking nothing. We watched the Hukoovu destroy both colonies. We know what they are capable of, we have shared this planet with them."

The security officer said, "And why shouldn't I believe that you aren't just trained by her to say what she wants?"

Trina shook her head. She could hardly believe what this man was saying. But she realized, in the end, it didn't matter. They could believe what they wanted to. They would eventually find out.

Trina said, "Look, if you want to believe some cockamamie idea that I made all of this up, that's fine. I'm sorry that you have chosen that."

The woman who had asked her the questions earlier spoke up. "I don't believe that—what you say makes a lot of sense."

"Dr. Miller…"

"What?"

"You are not trained in security issues."

"And you are not a trained anthropologist, are you?"

The Commander raised his arms, and shouted, "Look, I'm in charge, and I am making no conclusions at this moment. I want to see the recordings made of the… the Hukoovu, and I will talk with the Captain, and we'll go from there, alright? Everyone, you have a job to do, so do it."

Everyone except the anthropologist, one Security officer, and the Commander drifted away, back to their tasks.

Commander Rincón said, "Please show me these recordings."

Trina took out her tablet and showed them the recordings she'd made while on a trip with Litreela. They had flown over several times, and Trina had recorded them doing varied things, as well as sitting by the fires.

Trina said, "It's hard to tell how big they are, but look at the measurement indicators there." She pointed at one edge of the tablet, which had a scale.

Dr. Miller, the anthropologist said, "They are huge! I guess that makes sense, given that the gravity is so much weaker here."

Trina said, "When I first saw them, I was astounded. Seeing them on the ground is scary."

Dr. Miller smiled said, "No wonder you climbed a tree."

Trina nodded, feeling glad that the anthropologist believed her. "By the way, my name is Liane." She stuck out her hand, and Trina shook it.

The Security officer said, "May I take this tablet with the recordings?"

Trina had suspected that they would want the tablet, so she had copies of everything elsewhere.

"Sure, take it. You'll also find a journal of my time here, as well as lots of information about what I've learned about this planet. Feel free to read it all, I'm not hiding anything."

He took it from her, and walked toward the shuttle, and disappeared into it.

Liane said, "May I talk with the…"

Trina said, "The Eeriv. They are free agents, and you don't need my permission."

Liane walked to Zolweeva and Litreela, who were perched on the ground a bit apart from the humans. They were out of earshot, so Trina could not hear their conversation. She turned to the Commander.

"Commander, I know you might not believe me…"

"Actually, I do believe you. But it's not my call. It's the Captain's. Besides moving, what can you suggest we do?"

"There isn't anything you can do, Commander. They will destroy the colony. First, this is their territory, and they protect it. Second, they… they don't have enough food to eat, and humans would be the biggest available meat source around. And they also took all of the food from the second colony stores. You should definitely place some sort of patrol in the hills west, so they can warn you of a coming attack. But from what I could tell, they are tougher than the weapons that the second colony had with them."

"This land you speak of beyond the forest, why is it safe?"

"It's safe because the Hukoovu never go near the forest, and there are cliffs to the north, cutting off access."

"Why don't they go into the forest?"

"That's a really good question, and it's hard to explain if you haven't been here a while. The trees are much more mobile than trees at home, and they do not like the Hukoovu, and they trap them when they enter the forest. It's true, the Hukoovu do not enter the forest, let alone go through it."

"Wow, really? That's fascinating. Anyway, what's east of that land?"

Trina smiled. "The ocean. I've seen it. It's really wonderful, and the water is less salty than the oceans on Earth. And it's quite swimmable."

The main Security officer came back, with four other officers in tow. Trina did not like the look of this.

"Commander, the Captain would like to speak with you immediately."

He nodded and went toward the shuttle.

"Ms. Dewing, you are under arrest."

"Under arrest?"

"For sabotage of the second colony."

"You've got to be kidding me!"

"I am not kidding." He held something in his hands that Trina didn't recognize, and Trina realized she was in trouble. She at first wasn't sure what to do. The last thing in the world she wanted was be in captivity with these people, especially with the Hukoovu danger. She made a flash decision and ran toward Zolweeva and Litreela.

Trina shouted, "Zolweeva, go! Litreela, take me!"

Zolweeva launched into the air, and Litreela turned his back to her, and began to unfurl his wings. Trina heard three shots fired, and felt a pain in her back, and as she fell, shew saw Zolweeva fall to the ground. She tried to crawl toward him, then she felt a weight on her back, causing her excruciating pain. She blacked out.

She came to and looked up to see a ceiling. She looked around and saw that she was in a very small space, with medical instruments all around. She lifted up her right hand, only to find that it was chained to the bed. Her left hand was free at least. For now, she was alone.

She worried about Zolweeva and Litreela. She'd heard three shots, and she knew that at least one of them had hit her, and one hit Zolweeva. The last she'd seen he had been falling to the ground. She cursed herself. If she'd not let them come with her, he would not have gotten injured.

She was angry. Angry at the Security people for being such idiots, and angry at herself for not better preparing for this. She never imagined it happening this way, but she realized that she should have. It should have occurred to her that Security from *Precious Hope* would have reported her as a suspect. And given that reality, she would have known that it was going to be dangerous.

Well, there wasn't much she could do about it now. She was injured, and she was in captivity. She lay there, brooding, until she heard someone enter the room. She looked to see someone she'd not met before.

"Hi Trina. My name is Dr. Adanna Oza, but you can just call me Adanna. You suffered a gunshot wound, but luckily it didn't hit anything critical. You lost some blood, but you'll be fine soon enough."

"How are my companions?"

"One of them was badly injured. A number of others of their species took them away. I don't know more than that."

She was relieved. At least Zolweeva was in the care of the Eeriv, and it sounded like Litreela didn't get injured.

"Thank you. Where am I?"

"You are in the shuttle's medical bay. You'll have to be moved soon, although I'm not exactly sure where they will put you. I'm sorry that this happened. I had a long talk with Liane Miller, who is trying to advocate on your behalf with the captain. This whole thing is causing somewhat of a problem."

"I've never understood why I was a suspect in the first place. But I can see why, given that I was a suspect, that the fact that I am the only survivor might seem suspicious."

"Well, from my perspective, they are being paranoid. I can't even believe there were any saboteurs at all. But both of these colonies were destroyed, I guess perhaps I can't blame them too much for being paranoid."

"We need to get them to move the colony placement!"

"Some are suspicious that you are leading us into a trap."

"What? If I wanted to do something, couldn't I just do it here? That's nuts!"

"I agree. But I said: they are paranoid."

Another voice said, "Choose to believe we are being paranoid, Dr. Oza, or believe we are doing what is in the best interest of this colony."

The Security Chief appeared in her view.

Trina said, "What's in the best interest of the colony is to move it. I'm sorry you don't believe me. I might like the idea of being able to say, 'I told you so,' except that we might not be alive when I could say it."

The doctor walked out, and she was left alone with the Security chief.

"Ms. Dewing, as soon as the doctor gives her permission, we will be moving you outside, and we have many questions for you."

"I am happy to answer whatever questions you have, Mr…"

"Lieutenant Emerson Holcomb."

"Lieutenant Holcomb. Really. I'll answer anything."

"Well, you can start with why you wanted to run."

"You wanted to arrest me! Why wouldn't I run? Being in captivity is not something I want, especially given the danger coming. I don't want to die, sir."

"But if you cooperated, you could prove your innocence."

"Why should I have to prove my innocence? I have never understood why I was considered suspect in the first place—it never made sense to me."

Lieutenant Holcomb laughed. "The 'accident' that killed your parents was found to be a deliberate act."

"And that matters why? You think I killed my parents?"

"No. We think that your employers used that as cover."

Trina just couldn't see how this made any sense, so she was honest.

"Who are 'my employers?' That doesn't make any sense. The only employer I have right now is Kepler Exploratory, just like you. How do you know this act was targeting my parents? There were hundreds of people there."

He smiled this very sinister smile. "We know you are New Order, you just need to admit it."

"New Order? They didn't come into being until after we launched! I'd never heard of them until I fixed the receiver and started getting the transmissions from Earth."

"Don't lie. You know the New Order has been in place for many, many years, and they have been spying on these missions, and placing their agents on them. Our assumption is that you are going to help claim Johannes for the New Order."

Trina didn't quite know what to say. He seemed so sure of himself. How could she possibly convince him otherwise? She was spent.

She said quietly, "I don't know why you think I'm an agent of the New Order."

He said, "Oh, we have lots of evidence. We'll talk more when you are feeling better." He turned and left her alone. She felt hopeless. She figured they were ready to railroad her. She had no idea what was in store.

The doctor came back a few times and brought her some food and drink. Trina slept on and off. She dreamed about Zolweeva and her forest home. She woke, missing both.

"Hey." She looked to see Liana standing near her.

"Hi. Do you know how Zolweeva is?"

"He's doing fine. Litreela came by to tell me the news."

"Security didn't…"

"No, security doesn't really care about them. I told Litreela what happened to you."

"Thanks."

"He's worried."

"I'm worried."

"I've been talking with Commander Rincón and the Captain. The Commander is on my side, but the captain is on Security's side. But it's looking like the captain would be willing to let you go after interrogation, with the promise that you or the Eeriv will not come within a certain distance of the colony."

"What about moving the colony?"

"The captain is adamant. The colony will stay here."

Trina sighed. "I'm sorry."

"It's alright. It will work out."

"You believe that?"

She nodded. Clearly, she was not telling Trina everything. Trina let it go.

Trina lost track of days, but eventually, when she could stand and walk on her own, she was taken outside, then into a yurt. Lieutenant Holcomb was sitting in a chair behind a makeshift desk. There was nowhere for Trina to sit, so she kept standing.

"Ms. Dewing, the Captain is willing to have you released, once you answer some of our questions."

"I'll answer whatever you ask."

"Tell me about this 'attack' you say happened to the second colony."

Trina started at the beginning—when they had landed and found the remains of the first colony. She told them about building the colony, and then recounted that horrible day.

"So, you say that there was disagreement about the fate of the first colony?"

"There was. Some people didn't think sabotage was the best explanation."

"Who said that?"

"Who?"

"Yes. Who did you hear this from?"

"Well, my friend Bridgit had found some human remains, and there were arguments between Science and Security about them."

"Bridgit…?"

Trina thought and realized she didn't remember Bridgit's last name.

"Sorry, I don't remember her last name. But I think she was the only Bridgit on the ship."

"Why was there disagreement about the remains?"

"Science said that they determined that there were knife wounds, and there were teeth marks on the bones. But Bridgit thought the teeth marks were too large for scavengers. Of course, we know now that they had been eaten by the Hukoovu."

The Lieutenant was silent. Maybe he was beginning to believe her story?

He asked her more about her time among the Eeriv, and then he rapidly switched tacks.

"Did you go to church?"

"Church? In the colony?"

"No, on Earth."

"My parents did, and I occasionally accompanied them, when they asked me to. I didn't like it much, though."

"They attended 'Church of the New Day' didn't they?"

"Yes. How did you know that?"

"Let's just say we know a lot of things. You didn't like it?"

"I just told you that."

"Did you ever talk to the pastor?"

"Maybe once…"

As she pictured him, she realized why the President on those old transmissions seemed vaguely familiar to her. He was the pastor of that church! She then understood all of this. She felt some relief to finally understand the suspicion, even though it was unwarranted.

Trina said, "I thought what he preached was nuts, and I still think it now. I'd never do anything for him."

"Well, of course you were trained to say that."

Trina was silent. He said, "Did you know that he was a major investor in CalSpace?"

"What? He was an investor in CalSpace Tours?"

"Yes. And you know that CalSpace became the official space company of the New Order."

"I'm sorry. I had no idea he was an investor. Really! How can I convince you that I'm innocent?"

"You cannot. I am already convinced of your guilt. However, the Captain and First Officer are not. Therefore, we are releasing you on one condition."

"And that is?"

"That you stay far away. We will have a patrol on the east outskirts of the colony. If you, or any of your friends..." he spat, "come within shooting distance, they will shoot to kill."

"Alright, I will obey that. But you must move the colony!"

He laughed. "No. We are not moving the colony. According to the probe, and the initial Science reports, as well as early reports from the first two colonies, this is prime land, perfect for our needs."

"The plains beyond the forest are just as good."

"The captain has said the colony is not moving, and I have no more to discuss with you about it. You are free to go."

Trina threw up her hands. "Fine. Your death sentence."

She walked out of the yurt, where Liana was waiting, holding her pack for her.

"Hey. Here's your pack."

"Thanks. Look, you've got to find a way..."

"Don't worry, Trina. I'm on it."

"Come into the forest whenever you want. There will be help there."

Liana nodded. "Bye Trina. I'll see you again, I promise."

Trina smiled, and they hugged. "Bye Liana. Good luck."

Trina walked toward the forest, seeing various colony members watching her walking away. She reached the security perimeter, which was currently just a few officers scattered in an arc marked by tape.

One said, as she passed. "If we see you, or one of those creatures, we shoot to kill."

"I've been told that. Don't worry. It won't happen."

She kept walking, and finally made it into the forest. She climbed one of the first trees she found and looked for sign of any Eeriv. Soon, she saw one flying towards her. Litreela landed on a branch close to her.

"Treena, you are alright?"

"I've been better, Litreela. How is Zolweeva?"

"He is healing."

"I am glad to hear that. Take me to see him?"

Litreela cooed, and she climbed on his back.

They arrived at the home of Zolweeva and Keeliza, and Trina saw Zolweeva lying in a mound of cloth. Keeliza was perched near him. He looked towards her as she walked in.

"Treena! You have escaped. It is so nice to see you looking well."

"Zolweeva, I am so sorry about what happened to you!"

"It was not your fault, Treena."

"I feel responsible—I should have predicted…"

"Treena, do not worry. I will be fine soon. The healer has said I'll be ready to fly in a few days."

"I'm glad to hear that. They released me, but no Eeriv can come near the colony. And nor can I."

Litreela said, "I have warned everyone, and we will be keeping watch for the Hukoovu."

"What can we do once they attack?"

Litreela said, "I have some ideas I'm working on. We'll discuss it soon."

Trina nodded. Litreela was a smart and practical Eeriv. She looked forward to hearing what he came up with.

"I'll let you rest, Zolweeva. Keeliza, please let me know if there is anything I can do to help."

Keeliza cooed, and she and Litreela left the house, and Litreela flew Trina home.

Journal Entry, January 20, 2145

I don't quite know what to write today. It's been a horrible time. My plans are completely in disarray. I feel like I should have realized that Security from the first colony would have reported me as a suspect. I also wish I had known that my parent's pastor was connected to CalSpace Tours. I would have never applied for that job, had I known. I never liked him—he always gave me the creeps, and now I know why.

So, anyway, the colony isn't moving, and the only thing we can hope to do is save as many of them as possible, once the Hukoovu attack. I don't even know how, but I will ask Litreela's help in figuring it out.

I'm glad there seem to be some reasonable people in the colony. I like Dr. Liana Miller. She seems like a really nice person, and smart, too. I like the way she thinks, and it seems we can get along well. I'll do whatever I can to help make sure she survives, with as many others as I can.

Today, I feel lonelier than I have ever felt, even having been here alone all this time. I guess it's because now I know there are humans here again, but I can't spend time with them, or get to know them. I feel exiled, and all I did was try to help them.

Litreela has tried to soothe me, but it isn't working. It will be a while before I can get used to this new reality.

Third Destruction: January 2145

When Trina had gotten home, and settled down, she finally unpacked her pack and found a small communicator that hadn't been there before. She was glad Liana had put it there—it would be good for them to be in touch. She turned it on, plugged it into her solar array, and left it on her desk. The Eeriv would be watching to see if there was an attack by the Hukoovu. So, either way, Trina would know if an attack happened.

She tried to get back into her routine, but she realized that she didn't need to do the things she had been doing all this time to prepare for the arrival of the new colony. It made her feel adrift. She knew that she had friends in the new colony, but there was nothing she could do to stop what was inevitably going to happen to them.

She looked forward to hearing from Litreela about his plans for saving as many as possible from the Hukoovu. Trina wondered what he had in mind. In the meanwhile, how was she going to spend her time? She still had a lot of the Eeriv language to learn, although she despaired of it. Litreela had wanted her help in translating some of the Eeriv works on history and philosophy to English, and that could certainly take up her time. Somehow, even though there were now other humans on Johannes, she felt more alone than she'd felt before.

A loud beep came from the communicator.

"Trina? Are you there? It's Liana."

Trina pushed the transmit button.

"Yes, I'm here. Hi!"

"I can't talk long, I just wanted to make sure you'd found the communicator."

"I did. Thanks. It's good to hear from you." It was good to hear from her.

"I'll keep you posted. We're getting another shipment of crew today. Everyone will be down in a matter of days."

"Litreela has a plan to help when the Hukoovu attack. I haven't heard the details yet, but when I do, I'll let you know of them."

"Thanks. Bye for now."

"Bye, Liana."

She realized that one way she could spend her time was to finish her mapping and inventory of the valley beyond the forest, to help prepare the way for a new colony there. Out of curiosity, she went to the narrow-band receiver, and turned it on. There was nothing—no more signal from Earth, just like it had been for years now. She guessed that they had not been able to get enough power to transmit.

Two days later, she was sitting in her room, recording a journal entry, when Litreela cooed from her porch.

"Come in Litreela. Hello!" He walked in, then hopped on the guest perch.

"Hi Treena. How are you feeling?"

"Physically better, for sure. But I'm still angry and sad. But I'm glad to be back home. How is Zolweeva?"

"He is much better. He should be able to fly tomorrow."

"That is good. I'm happy that he is better."

"I have some plans to discuss with you."

"Yes, please!"

"When the Hukoovu attack, the colony will be too busy to bother with guarding the forest side of the camp."

"Agreed."

"Also, you have a friend inside?"

"Yes, she gave me a way to communicate with her."

"Ah, good. So, we have been watching from the western cliffs…"

"You can see the Hukoovu march from there?"

"Yes. We will have about ten eerfs of notice." Trina nodded and remembered that an eerf was about ten minutes of her time. They would have just over an hour and a half notice before the attack.

"How do they know the colony is there?"

"They have a very keen sense of smell, and the prevailing wind is from the east to the west."

"I wonder why it took them so long to attack the colonies, and I wonder how long it will take them to attack this one."

"Perhaps their experience will make them bolder."

"I guess that's possible. Alright, so when the Hukoovu march…"

"We have thirty volunteers who will fly over the colony once the attack starts, and pick up people, either on the ground or in the trees."

"Won't that be dangerous?"

"If we are picking people up on the ground yes."

"So, it would be best if as many people as possible climbed the trees."

"Yes, Treena, that would be safest."

"How fast do the Hukoovu move?"

"It would be hard for a human to outrun them, if that's the question."

"Yes, that was my question." That made sense to Trina. From her experience during the last attack, they did seem fast.

"We should not depend on many of your people being able to outrun the Hukoovu."

Trina nodded.

"OK, Litreela. I'll let my friend know of the plans."

He cooed. "I have some questions, Treena, if you don't mind."

"Of course. What is it?"

"Why did they capture you?"

"They suspect me of sabotage. Remember I talked about that before?"

"Ah, yes. But these are not the same people. How did they know?"

"Security from the second colony had sent a report back with my name in it. And someone had done some research on the church I went to when I was a child."

"Remind me what a church is, Treena?"

"A church is a religious organization, specifically of Christian religion. Apparently, the leader of the church my parents attended has now become the head of that 'New Order' organization. And he was an investor in the major competitor to Kepler Exploratory. And these folks suspected the 'New Order' of sabotage."

"But to suspect you, Treena…"

"They don't know me, so all they have to go on is their suspicions."

"I'm so sorry, Trina. What's a competitor?"

"On Earth, when I was there, there were groups of people who formed 'companies'.

These companies offered specific services. Some companies offered the same services, so they competed with each other for customers. Kepler Exploratory, which was part of Solar Exploratory, as well as CalSpace, offered space tourism."

"Tourism?"

"That's when you take trips to see things that you've never seen before. Like going into space."

Litreela was silent a moment. "Why would two groups offer the same service?"

"So they could make money."

"We've talked about money before, and I've written about it, but I'm still not completely sure I understand it. But basically, they competed with each other because they both wanted to prosper."

Trina knew that the Eeriv didn't use money, or an abstraction of resources of any kind.

"Yes, that's basically true."

"One more question, Treena."

"Sure, Litreela."

"You speak differently when you talk of Liana. I've never heard you speak quite the same. Is she a prospective mate?"

Trina was embarrassed. She didn't quite know what to say to that. The Eeriv generally spoke very plainly about the process of choosing mates, much more plainly than human beings ever did.

"Um, I don't know, Litreela."

"Did I ask something wrong?"

"No, no Litreela, it's alright."

"I hope I didn't make you uncomfortable."

"No. Not at all." She was uncomfortable, but it was more about the fact that he had made something that was in her subconscious, conscious.

About fifteen days later, Trina heard the beep of the communicator.

"Hi, Trina here."

"Hey Trina, it's Liana."

"Hey, I was worried about you—I hadn't heard from you in so long, and I was afraid to initiate contact. I'm glad to hear from you."

"I'm sorry! Things are pretty crazy here right now. I finally got out to do some reconnaissance east of the camp. I figured I'd use this alone time to call you. How are you doing, and how is Zolweeva?"

"I'm alright, mostly healed up. Zolweeva has been flying for a while now. He's doing well."

"Ah, that's good to hear."

"I have heard Litreela's plans."

"You have? What are they?"

"Litreela and others are watching the Hukoovu from the western cliffs, and they will have advance warning of the attack."

"How much warning?"

"About an hour and a half. That's a good hour more than your scouts."

"Indeed. So, what then?"

"Well, since the Eeriv will be shot on sight before the attack, we have to wait until after the attack starts. Thirty of the Eeriv have volunteered to rescue people from the colony."

"Thirty?"

"If we could get in beforehand, it would be better. But if you have people climb the trees, the Hukoovu can't get up them."

"Well, I have something to tell you that will make rescue easier."

"And that is?"

"There are about forty of us that are ready to defect. We could leave well before the Hukoovu attack. Then there would be fewer people to rescue."

"Really?"

"Yes. It's been a real nightmare here. We've been working hard to convince the Captain that you are right, that these creatures are a danger, but he refuses to believe it. But I want the colony to move, now, before we are in danger, and there are enough of us that want to do that. We are planning our defection now."

"When do you think you'll make your move?"

"In the next five days."

"How can I help?"

"We need guidance through the forest."

"Of course! Just tell me when you're planning to make it to the edge of the forest, and I'll meet you there."

"Great! And thanks for the details on the rescue plans. There are a couple of folks who are basically on our side, but don't want to defect. I'll leave the communicator with them, and you can use it to warn them of the attack by the Hukoovu, although I honestly doubt that the captain would take it seriously."

"Well, we can do what we can, right? Remember, stash as many amino acid supplements as you can, and I hope there are some chemists among the defectors."

"There are, and we're all over that. OK, I gotta go. Bye for now."

"Bye."

Trina sighed. She could sense a lot of tension in Liana's voice. She was a little surprised that forty people wanted to defect! That was a good thing, and perhaps meant that they could rescue more people. And it also meant that Liana would be out of harm's way.

Six days later, Trina was trudging through the forest, with thirty-five people in tow. Liana was walking next to her.

"We'll follow this trail, which goes to the river, and we can follow the river from there."

"Where did this trail come from, Trina? I thought that the Eeriv didn't spend time on the ground, and the Hukoovu never came into the forest."

"Both of those things are true. I made and maintained this trail myself over the past eight years, in preparation for the new colony's arrival. I thought that if you did indeed land where the previous colony landed, we'd need a good path to get through to the valley beyond."

"Wait, you spent eight years preparing for this?"

"More than nine, actually, once I started to get my bearings. I fixed electronics, cataloged and tested plants and animals as food sources, tested a few crops, made trails through the forest, created storage depots, mapped out the valley, etc. It's been a busy time."

Liana was quiet, and Trina didn't know what was on her mind, but she didn't press her as they kept walking.

Trina said, "So, how did the whole defection thing go?"

Liana looked grim. "It was a nightmare. Security learned of the plan the day after I talked with you and threatened to put all of us back into cryosleep, which was pretty obviously ridiculous—they knew they didn't have the power to do that. The Captain decided to just let us go. Some other members feel really betrayed by us. We didn't get to take a whole lot with us, we have enough supplements to last us a while, but we didn't get 1/3 of the supplies, by a long shot. But we do have a chemist."

"I've got a possible avenue to synthesize the amino acids. There is a plant that has high levels of pyruvate and threonine. But if there are enough supplements for a year or so, we can just grow crops. I'm not much of a farmer, but I managed to be able to grow some lettuce and kale, and I even planted some strawberries, which have been producing fruit."

"Wow, that's great. Did you recover seeds from the colony?"

"Yes. I built a storage yurt in the valley, and there are lots of seeds there. The Hukoovu badly damaged the containers but didn't take or eat the seeds. I scavenged other containers and put the seeds in them. Sadly, the embryos are all gone, since the attack destroyed the refrigeration."

Liana smiled and turned back and pointed. "See those four big boxes?"

"Yes."

"They are about 1/2 of the embryos."

"How did you manage that?"

"I explained that the Hukoovu attack would likely destroy the rest, and wouldn't they like an insurance policy? The lead of Animal Husbandry agreed, and also gave us enough solar panels to keep the refrigeration going. I don't think the captain knows that we have so many of them."

"I'm glad. I've wanted a dog for years, now."

"A dog?" Liana laughed.

"It was a childhood dream. Impossible for my family."

Liana was quiet and looked at Trina. Trina couldn't quite decipher the look, but it was not unpleasant.

They reached the river.

Trina said, "It's probably a good time to take a break for the night. The beginning of the valley is about a day's walk away. There is a dock over here…"

"Did you build that?"

"I did. See that boat?"

"Yes, is that yours?"

"Yes. I use it to go fishing."

"Fishing?"

"There is an aquatic animal that is a lot like fish, and tastes sort of like fish, I guess, although I only ever tasted fish once in my life. It's decent though, and plentiful. The Eeriv eat it. It was the first thing they gave me to eat after they rescued me."

"They are strictly hunter-gatherers, is that correct?"

"Yes. They actively chose not to pursue agriculture."

"Really?"

"Yes, really. Way back when, one particular individual thought it would lead to strife and separation of the Eeriv and counseled against it. They followed his counsel."

"How far did they get in science?"

"Well, their systems of thought are really differently arranged, and it's a real mix. I'd say they are pretty far beyond us in language and philosophy. They know their planet is round, and they know exactly what stars are, and it wasn't a super big surprise to them that they got visitors from another planet. They were almost expecting it."

"Interesting."

"And there is so much they have chosen not to pursue. They eschew technology beyond the basics, like their clay ovens, basic metalworking, and such. They have an amazing way with some plants—they can coax them to do astonishing things. They also decided not to pursue electricity, although they understand it."

Liana shook her head. "I will be spending the rest of my life studying them. So fascinating."

"They are already studying us. In the time before you got here, three books on human history were already written."

"How?"

"Well, information from my tablets, and interviews with me. So they aren't very good history books." Trina grinned. "But they are very curious about humans."

"Hrmmph. I don't know why. We're a pretty screwed up species."

Trina laughed. "They like humans."

"Even after we shot one of them?"

"Yes, it didn't really seem to faze them."

Everyone spread out, and they set up camp. Trina went out in the boat with Liana, and they caught five fish, enough for everyone. They cooked them over the fire someone had made.

Later that night, Trina and Liana were sitting by the fire, with a few other people. They were discussing how they were going to organize the spin-off colony. Trina stayed quiet and listened. She liked how Liana was emerging as a leader.

The next day, they walked along the river. Trina was walking next to Adanna Oza, the doctor that had tended her in the colony.

Adanna said, "This river reminds me of home."

Trina asked, "Where are you from?"

"I am from northern Minnesota. I lived by the Flambeau River. It was a lot like this when I was growing up, although by the time I'd left, it had become much more built up."

"I've never been to Minnesota. In fact, I've actually never been much of anywhere on Earth. I lived in Queens for a while, until our neighborhood got flooded out. Then I lived in the Bronx, then the Nevada launch facility, then here."

"How did you end up on the *Precious Hope?* Everyone on the *Calypso* had been in space before."

"My parents died when I was sixteen. They had a lot of debt from their parents, supposedly. They died in an accident, although I've now been told it wasn't an accident, and my parents didn't have as much debt as I'd been told they did. Anyway, my family sold my labor contract to LSI."

"Really? I'd heard rumors that Kepler had gotten some LSI folks, but I didn't believe it. LSI, and inherited debt, were outlawed pretty much the minute the world government was official, about seven years after you left. There was a huge debt jubilee."

"Well, I don't regret it. I mean, I'm sorry that my parents died, but I'm happy to have gotten to come here."

"I can understand that."

"How did you end up on *Calypso?*"

"My father was one of the investors. He really wanted me to go. He was afraid of what was going to happen on Earth. I think he was right."

Trina nodded. She wondered whether or not the transmissions from Earth were going to resume, or whether they would never hear from Earth again.

They trudged slowly along the river. It was easy to follow the river—Trina hadn't had to do too much work to maintain a trail—in many places, there were beaches and meadows along the river. The colonists were carrying a lot of equipment and had only a few robotic all-terrain carriers.

Finally, as the sun started to set, they reached the makeshift camp and storage yurt Trina had set up several years ago. She hadn't spent much time here in a while—but nothing seemed much the worse for wear.

She stayed for a few days, offering help where it made sense, giving advice where she knew things that the other colonists didn't yet. Litreela came by occasionally, to check in, and other Eeriv would visit as well. They were clearly curious about this group, and why it was different than the rest.

Finally, Trina decided to go home for a while. She bid Liana and others goodbye and let them know that she would be back. She flew back home with Litreela. They landed on her porch, and she climbed off of his back.

"Will you go back to them Treena?"

"Yes, Litreela. They could use my assistance. But it's nice to be home."

"Treena, why have only some moved to safety?"

"The Captain—he's the leader—he doesn't believe they are in danger. He thinks I cooked the whole thing up, and really, it was me who destroyed the colony."

"That sounds... that sounds far-fetched."

"It does to me too! But that's what they believe. The ones that left believe me, and think the colony is really in danger."

"Well, of course, you will be found to be correct."

Trina shrugged. "Yes but knowing that doesn't really make me feel much better."

"I understand." He switched to Eeriv. "A glorious rest/accompanies restores body/sunrise will see my eyes again, Treena."

"Goodnight, Litreela," Trina replied in English.

Litreela flew to his home, and Trina went inside. When she walked into the kitchen, she found that someone had left some very nice-looking food out for her. She shook her head in wonder. She had been here for ten years, and they still treated her like the best combination of a guest and family.

Days went by. She would spend a few days at home, then fly with Litreela to visit the colony in the valley. They were doing well. They had finished erecting all of the yurts they had brought with them and had begun to build some wooden structures from dead trees they had found at the edge of the forest. She had explained to Liana how the Eeriv honored the trees, and never used live ones, and how the trees treated the Hukoovu, who had killed live trees. She hoped that the colony would respect the trees as the Eeriv did.

She liked spending time with the colonists, but she also liked spending time at home, and with the Eeriv. She realized that at some point, she was going to have to make a choice, but for now, it was fine to go back and forth.

One morning, about forty days after the second colony was established, Trina was woken by an urgent shriek from the front of her house. She rose and walked out of her bedroom to see Litreela and Kileeza in her front room.

"The Hukoovu are marching, Treena," Kileeza said.

"OK, I will let everyone know. Are the volunteers assembled?"

"Yes, Treena. Would you like to accompany me?"

"No, Litreela—that would take up a space. You don't need me there."

Litreela cooed. "We will bring everyone we can rescue to the edge of the forest. You'll meet us there?"

"I will, yes."

They both left, and Trina quickly got dressed. She first wanted to communicate with the main colony, to let them know that an attack was coming. She had talked briefly with a man named Gaynor, who was sympathetic to the break-off colony, but he didn't want to leave.

"Gaynor, please come in." There was nothing.

"Gaynor!"

A muffled voice answered. "Trina? What's going on?"

"The attack is happening. The Hukoovu are marching. You have about an hour before they arrive. About thirty Eeriv are waiting at the edge of the forest for the attack to begin. They will attempt to rescue as many as possible. If you can convince the Captain…"

"Sorry, he won't budge. He's going to have to see these Hukoovu up close and personal before he relaxes the guard on the eastern side of the colony."

"Alright, well, as I said before, get as many people as possible into the trees. And if you can convince anyone to run to the forest now, that would be great."

"Roger."

There wasn't really anything else to say. Trina knew that the likelihood that anyone would go anywhere before the Hukoovu showed up was quite slim. She put in the channel for the new colony.

"Liana?" There was a pause.

"Trina? How are you? Are you coming back today?"

"The Hukoovu are marching. I let Gaynor know. I'll be at the edge of the forest, ready to lead the survivors to you. I imagine it will take us until the end of the day tomorrow to get there, depending on what happens."

"OK, we'll be ready for them. Be careful, Trina."

"Will do."

Trina grabbed some breakfast, packed a few things, and climbed down her tree to the floor of the forest. She quickly followed the trail she'd made to the edge and climbed up a tree at the edge to get a good view. Not far away were many Eeriv perched in trees, waiting for the attack.

She took out her binoculars and could see that the colony was in an uproar. She knew that the western scouts had made it back by now. Strangely, there were many more members of Security along the eastern side. She was puzzled for a minute, but then she realized that they must think that the marching of the Hukoovu were a ruse of some sort. She shook her head. It wouldn't matter one way or another.

She wasn't looking forward to watching the events unfold. She basically already knew what would happen, since she'd experienced it. She tried to piece together what they were thinking, based on what she could see. First, there was the added presence on the eastern side. Then, she could see a line of people on the western side. She wondered if they were going to try to actually greet the Hukoovu. She wondered whether the Hukoovu would be open to any kind of communication, or they would just go ahead and attack. She expected the latter. She knew, based on her experience and what the Eeriv said, they saw humans as a food source. That wasn't likely to make communication possible.

She could see a cloud of dust over the horizon. That would be the oncoming Hukoovu. As she watched, they came into view, moving quickly toward the colony. The line in front of them didn't move, until it was clear that the Hukoovu had no intention of stopping. Suddenly, everyone broke and ran, some climbing trees, others just running toward the forest. The Hukoovu were fast—they caught several people who were trying to run away.

Trina turned to see the Eeriv take off. She hoped that as many people as possible could make it into the trees, otherwise, there was no way they were going to survive this attack.

Trina could see one man stand right in the center of the colony, looking at the Hukoovu attack. She increased the magnification, and realized that it was the Security chief, Lieutenant Holcomb. He didn't move, and a nearby Hukoovu noticed him, and moved quickly toward him. The man raised his arm, which must have had a handgun in it. He stood his ground, shooting, but the Hukoovu didn't seem to at all react to being shot, and simply sliced the Lieutenant's head off with its long spear, and started to make a meal of him. Trina figured that perhaps, at the last moment, he wished that he had listened to her. She was sad, because this had all been so unnecessary.

Some Eeriv were already on their way back with survivors, so she climbed down the tree so she could meet them. There really wasn't much reason to keep watching the carnage. As she arrived at the place where her trail started, Keeliza and two other Eeriv dropped off three survivors, none of whom she knew.

"Hi. We're going to wait until the others are rescued, and then we have a bit of a walk to the new colony. They are getting ready for you."

One of them seemed very agitated, more than the rest.

"We need to save the embryos…"

"I'm sorry, but there is nothing you can do while the attack is happening. Perhaps we'll be lucky, and when the Hukoovu leave, we can…"

"Any interruption in the refrigeration will kill the embryos."

"I'm sorry, then. There isn't anything we can do. We have what the new colony took."

The man looked devastated.

"Who are you?" Trina asked.

"I'm Lennox Sturgis, head of Animal Husbandry. I'm glad we gave them half. I hope it is going to be enough."

"They seem to think it will be enough."

More and more survivors were arriving, and there was a lot of chatter and discussion. Some had managed to escape with packs, but most were empty-handed.

Finally, there were about forty people gathered, and Litreela said that there were no more alive. That meant more than thirty had been killed.

"Treena, the Hukoovu are still busy at the colony, but there are no more survivors. I'm sorry."

"Thank you, Litreela, for all of your help. Are you all alright?"

"Reteelo and Quizooli were injured slightly by Hukoovu blades. Otherwise, we are all fine."

Trina switched to Eeriv, doing the best she could. "Honor bound/gracious love my billowing heart/your great help/my care and heart to the hurt/my deep debt always."

Litreela said, "Open help we lovingly provide/the well full/our hearts greatly happy."

Litreela cooed and flew off.

Trina turned to the gathered crowd. "Alright everyone, please follow me. We have a long day and a half walk to the new colony."

A tall man she hadn't met stepped through the crowd.

"We can't leave yet."

"What do you mean?"

"We need to find more survivors, and also get supplies."

"It will be far too dangerous for you to go back there today. The Hukoovu will stick around until nightfall, when they will start their journey home. And I hate to tell you this, but you will find no more survivors."

"We need to go back. I suggest some of us camp here, then go back in the morning."

Trina sighed.

"Alright, that's up to you."

He shouted, "Strabo, Xanthe, Devangana, Aquila and Kerry, we'll stay here and camp."

Trina said, "I'd suggest, just for extra safety, that you camp a little bit into the forest. Actually, there's a nice little meadow about 10 minutes from here, along the way."

He nodded.

"OK, let's go."

No one else seemed in the mood to question her or ask her anything. They all seemed too stunned by what had just happened and were following along. She didn't know who the man was who wanted to stay behind, but she knew he must have some authority, to tell others to stay with him.

They arrived at the small meadow, and Trina gave the ones who were staying instructions on how to make it to the valley. Then, the rest of them kept walking. They found their way to the river and stopped to camp.

Trina did some fishing and instructed several people on how to find some edible plants, since there was very little food among the supplies people managed to grab quickly. A small group of people were sitting around the fire, late into the night with Trina, who was far from ready to go to sleep after such a day.

A woman, whose name she had learned was Dorine, came by to sit around the fire with the rest of the sleepless.

"I can't quite believe what happened."

Trina couldn't think of anything to say to that statement. The woman seemed to realize suddenly how what she'd said would sound to Trina.

"I'm sorry we didn't believe you. I can't imagine having survived that alone."

"Well, I wasn't alone. The Eeriv took really good care of me."

"They seem like interesting creatures."

"They are."

"They smell weird, though."

"Really? I never really noticed that."

"Well, you smell weird too. It might be something you're all eating. I do have a very sensitive nose."

"Well, then, perhaps we'll all start to smell weird." They all laughed.

Trina began, finally, to feel a bit sleepy. She got up, bid her fireside companions goodbye, and went to where she'd put her stuff. She laid out the bedroll she'd made a long time ago for trips just like this and fell promptly to sleep.

She was awoken by the sound of people stirring. They prepared a somewhat meager breakfast from last night's leftovers, and some supplies, and took off walking along the river.

Journal Entry, April 10, 2145

I have just gotten back from spending a little time at the new colony. Liana and her crew did an amazing job of preparing for the survivors, but there is already some discord between the two groups.

I helped as I could, but in reality, this colony doesn't really need me. I'd already given a tablet with all of my findings to the assistant head of Science, who defected with Liana. They have their own plans for setting up the colony, and I feel a little strange about it.

It's not that I don't feel welcome. Liana especially is happy to have me around and likes it when I spend time there. And I like spending time with her. But I wasn't a part of the ship, I didn't train with any of these people, and I don't feel exactly like I fit in.

At the same time, it seems silly for me to keep living in the forest with the Eeriv, when there is a colony full of humans not so far away. I don't know why I feel so at odds. Ten years away from humans has made contact with them somehow more complicated that I thought it used to be.

I'd like to invite Liana to my home, so she can see how I've been living, and meet more Eeriv. I know that she'd appreciate it.

New Colony: April, 2145

The new colony had been quite prepared for the arrival of the survivors. There were tents and yurts for people to stay in, plenty of food and supplies. There was not a small amount of grumbling from the original defectors. Most of the leaders of the colony, including the Captain, First Officer, and Security Chief had not survived. Several heads of teams, such as Logistics, Animal Husbandry, and Agronomy had, but the colony of defectors had set up their own systems and teams, and expected the survivors to fit in. The survivors expected the structure of the original colony to be maintained.

Trina spent some time in the colony over the next few months, and assisted as she could, but there wasn't really a place for her. She wasn't quite sure how to fit in, especially given the current strife. One day, she was sitting with Liana.

"I don't know what to do. I'm not sure I should stay. First, I can't stand the fighting. When are people going to calm down? It's been months, now."

"I don't know, Trina. We are in a bit of a stalemate at the moment, and the only saving grace is that we have so much work to do."

"Why is everyone being so intransigent?"

"Well, we feel like we believed what was coming, and did what was necessary to assure the survival of the colony. The others feel like they did what was needed, and they didn't 'leave their posts,' which is the current parlance for us."

"They don't admit that if you hadn't done what you did, everyone would be in far worse shape than you are?"

"No, they can't admit that, and I can sort of understand it. Sort of."

Trina shook her head. "Plus, it feels like people act really aloof towards me. I think they might resent me."

"They don't resent you, Trina, they are intimidated."

"Intimidated?"

"Yes! That comes as a surprise to you?"

"What did I do to be intimidating?"

"You survived, you are brilliant, you have friends on this planet that aren't human, you did a shitload of work for us, and people can see that."

Trina was silent. She didn't know quite what to say.

She asked Liana quietly, "Do I intimidate you?"

Liana smiled and touched Trina's hand. "A little."

"Will you come home with me sometime? I'd like you to see where I lived for all this time."

"I'd love to."

"OK, I'll get Litreela to bring a companion, and you can also get to fly."

"That would be fun!" Liana was grinning.

The next day, there was a big meeting, to try and iron out the differences between the two sides. Trina didn't have much hope. She was sitting on the outskirts, listening to the arguments. The most senior ranking officer from the ship, who had stayed behind, had been trying for weeks to assert his authority, but it was authority only some people followed. Liana was considered the main leader of the defectors, mostly because she'd organized the group. She was resented most by those who stayed. She tried her best to be conciliatory, but it didn't seem to help.

At one moment, as a shouting match between the senior ranking officer and one of the defectors reached an almost deafening level, Trina had an idea, and decided there was nothing to lose. She pushed her way to the front.

She said very loudly, "I have an idea!" No one heard her. She said it again, louder, and finally the din quieted.

The senior officer looked at her with an unreadable look.

"What is it?"

"It's time for all of you to just start over. It's clear that each side will never agree to follow the other. So you need to start from scratch. I suggest that you all nominate people to serve on a council. I don't know, maybe a council of five or six, something like that. And the person who gets the most votes becomes the leader of the council. The council will sort of be like a representative government for everyone."

There was silence for longer than felt comfortable to Trina. Finally, the senior officer said to Liana, "Would that be agreeable to you?"

Liana nodded. "Yes, it's a great idea."

Liana turned to the crowd. "Any objections?" There were none.

Liana said, "OK, I suggest that everyone gets to nominate five people, and the five people with the most votes sit on the council."

The senior officer said, somewhat quietly, "I'd like it if people can put more than one vote for a person."

Liana said, "That's agreeable, and fair. Each person has five votes, which they can use in any way they'd like."

Trina walked back to the outskirts of the crowd during the logistical part. She wanted to stick around to see what happened, but it was about time for her to go home. She'd been in the colony for almost a week, and she was homesick, and missed spending time with Litreela.

She sat down with her back to one of the trees near the edge of the colony. She was currently learning to read and write Eeriv. It was quite a challenge for her. She'd spent some time with one of the colonists who was a linguist, and they had been quite fascinated by the language.

Trina was interrupted when she saw movement at the edge of her vision. She looked up to see Liana, looking at her with a grin.

She said, "Ah, you won. I'm not surprised."

"Ah, no, I didn't win. I mean, I'm on the council, but one person got more votes than I did."

"Really? Johnson?"

Liana laughed. "No, he's on the council, too."

"Then who?"

"You."

Trina was stunned. "Me?! Wait, what?"

"Yes, you got the most votes. You are the head of the council."

"But… but, I'm not even part of the colony!"

"You are now. That is, if you want it. I told them you might refuse."

Trina put down the book. "Liana…"

Liana sat down next to her and put her arm around her shoulder.

"I know you love the Eeriv, Trina, but I think it's time for you to find your home among your own species now. Don't you think?"

"Give me some time? A few days?"

"Sure."

Trina went home and spent just a day thinking about it. She understood why they chose her, although she didn't really feel confident of her ability to lead them. But the fact that she got more votes than even Liana suggested to her that they had confidence in her, and that was probably enough.

She would miss being here. She wondered if she could still keep it and use it as a retreat when she needed to.

She heard a gentle coo on her porch, and she looked out to see Litreela and Zolweeva standing there. She motioned for them to come in.

Litreela said, "Have you decided, Treena?"

"I have. I'm going to agree to lead the colony."

Zolweeva said, "They are wise to choose you."

Trina smiled. "Thank you, Zolweeva."

Zolweeva cooed, then said, "There really isn't anything to thank me for, Treena. I'm just telling the truth."

Trina said, "Do you think I could keep this house? I don't want to inconvenience anyone."

Zolweeva said, "We would want you to keep this house, Treena. It inconveniences no one."

"Thank you, Zolweeva. That makes it easier for me to think about moving to the colony, knowing that I can always come back."

Litreela said, "Can I go pick up Liana now?"

Trina smiled. She had told Litreela on the flight back yesterday that she'd wanted Liana to come visit, and Litreela almost seemed more eager than Trina.

"Sure, if she's available, ask her."

Litreela walked out and took off from the porch.

"How is Keeliza? I haven't seen much of her lately."

"She's been asked by the elder council to spend time with another clan. Every 100 years or so we share everything we've learned with each other. It's time for this particular clan and ours to meet."

"How many clans do you meet with?"

"There are ten clans within one day's flight. Mostly to the north, but there are two clans to the south."

"Are there clans further away?"

"Yes, of course. There are clans that are many days flight away, but we never see them."

"That is by choice?"

"Yes. It is the way we always have done things."

In a few hours, just as Trina was getting dinner ready, Litreela returned with Liana. Liana entered into her house.

"Hey Trina!"

"Hello, Liana." They hugged. Trina was glad she was here.

"Make yourself comfortable."

Litreela said in an odd voice, "I will leave you now."

"Thank you, Litreela, for bringing me here."

"You are very welcome, Liana. Enjoy your stay." Litreela cooed, then walked out, and took off.

"Trina, this is an amazing house. It was grown?"

"Yes. There are Eeriv who know how to coax the trees to make shapes they want. See that door?"

"Yes."

"I watched it happen. This Eeriv put a larger and larger stone into a small crevice in the wood that got bigger by the moment. Eventually, she started to use a frame, and then there was the door. No cutting or burning, no nails or screws. The entire structure of the house is made that way."

"This furniture is interesting."

"Well, the table is theirs - you can see by how tall it is. But the rest—the smaller tables, the couch, the stools and chairs—I made those."

"Ah, I see. I was trying to understand why the table looked so different than everything else."

"That's because they really know how to build furniture, and I don't."

Liana laughed. "Actually, you didn't do such a bad job."

She sat on the couch. "Comfy."

Trina said, "Dinner is almost ready. Let me go finish it."

Liana got up and followed Trina into the kitchen.

"Wow, this is cool. Is this all theirs?"

"Mostly. The tables, stove, clay jars and most of the plumbing are all theirs. I rigged a solar hot water heater on the roof, and the grey plastic tubing carries the hot water. I put that together."

"They don't use hot water?"

"Nope. They wash their utensils and such in sand, then cold water. They don't bathe—they groom themselves and each other. They do sometimes swim in the river."

Trina said, "Dinner's ready. You hungry?"

Liana nodded, and helped Trina bring everything into the front room.

She said, "This all looks so delicious."

"That flat, thick leaf, there? It's really good. The Eeriv can't eat it, but we can. There are quite a few things I cataloged that we can eat, and they can't. And, of course, there are some things that they can eat that we can't."

"That makes sense. So I still can't understand why they don't use hot water. They really seem to eschew technology, even when they could easily do it."

"They aren't driven in the same way as we seem to be. They are happy living as they have lived in the forest for pretty much all of their history, from what I can tell."

"I will be studying them for my whole life."

"Litreela will be happy about that."

Liana looked puzzled. "Why Litreela?"

"Well, he chose not to take a mate, but to spend his time with me. We've done a lot together, but now that I'll be leading the council, I won't have a lot of time. I feel bad for him, but he insists he did the right thing for himself."

"I can see making that choice. I mean…"

"What?"

Liana said quietly, "You are a pretty compelling person to spend time with."

Two days later, she was standing next to Litreela, Keeliza and Liana near the new colony.

Litreela cooed. "Days and house empty/loss and no loss/great gladness of place/flying together wonderful future ahead."

Trina said in English, "Thanks, Litreela. It's important for me to do this, but I will miss you terribly. You'll visit often, and I will see you sometimes at my home?"

"You will always be in my heart, Treena, and I will visit often."

Liana said, "Thanks Litreela and Keeliza for giving us a ride. And of course we can't begin to thank you for all that the Eeriv have done for us."

Keeliza said, "No thanks are needed, Leeana. We are happy. We look forward to a long friendship between our clan and yours."

They flew off, and Liana and Trina walked back to the colony, hefting a lot of Trina's stuff.

"Ready, Trina?"

"No, but we might as well get started."

About the Author

Maxwell has been a science fiction fan since he could read. He has written and published poetry, creative nonfiction, and technical writing. He has self-published a number of science fiction novels. Maxwell lives and writes in Northern California.

Connect with him online:

Twitter: http://twitter.com/pearlbear
Web: http://author.maxwellpearl.com